WILDLING

MIDNIGHT SUN 2

LYNN BURKE

WILDLING

A wildling, Ma always called me, born of nature, feral as a fox.

I made a promise to her on her deathbed to look after my heartless Pa, but eight years later, he brings another woman to our homestead in the wilds of Alaska, testing my determination to honor Ma's memory.

Saige is timid. Beautiful. Unthreatening and desperate for affection, consuming my mind and drawing me in.

I should flee—for both our safety.

But I have nothing to my name, and leaving as winter approaches means certain death, no matter my survival skills.

Pa crosses a line, and the wildling inside me rises like a bear on its hind legs, instinctively needing to show dominance.

This time, I won't fail to protect the one I love, no matter the cost—even if it means breaking my promise and shedding blood.

1

SAIGE

My sneaker I wore for work didn't get kicked under my bed where it pushed against the wall. Sitting back on my haunches from having looked, I eyed the rest of my room with its single bookshelf, old bureau, and bed stand. Everything sat in its usual place.

Nothing littered the old carpet covering the floor.

Rummaging my parents' house beyond my bedroom door, keeping their mess away from my personal space wasn't an option. Hoarders, the both of them, and Mom's yappy dog loved shoes. The chances of me finding that sneaker?

Absolutely zero.

Asking either of them for help would prove just as futile. Since I could remember, Mom hadn't seemed to give two shits about me. Same with Dad.

"Damnitalltohell." Still grumbling, I stood, hands on hips, chewing the inside of my lip, and wracking my brain.

Spring had hit our area of Alaska, but sandal and flip-flop weather lay weeks away, and my lone pair of heeled boots would kill my feet long before my five-hour shift ended at the farm supply store I'd been working at for six years.

The bank envelope I kept taped to the back of my bed stand held enough cash to purchase a new pair, but I hoarded my dollar bills like Dad did pizza boxes and plastic beer pack rings. Not that I saved for anything specific. Since neither of my parents could get jobs with their so-called disabilities, and also couldn't get approved for government assistance, I paid the bills. I kept a roof over our heads. I brought home the staple groceries to see us through.

Where the hell they got cash for takeout, beer, and the pills they popped, I had no clue.

I never got a word of thanks, either.

They'd made their beds long before Mom had brought me into the world—not that they could find said bed beneath the clothing and rubbish filling the other bedroom in our small house.

Dad slept on the couch, Mom in her recliner.

Both claimed I'd been nothing but a burden since being born. Somehow, they overlooked the fact I went above and beyond to support them—all in hopes of a word of affirmation, an affectionate pat on the head.

It's as though they floated through their drugged-out days, siphoning off me rather than the government who acknowledged them as much as my parents did me—not at all.

Wasted energy, wasted hopes, on my part. My constant failures had weakened my resolve to make them *see* me. Appreciate me.

Depression had made me her bitch over the winter, no matter how hard I tried to keep my chin up.

Both still snored as I quietly made my way into the kitchen with a heavy heart. I traversed the path I cleared every night once they passed out, scanning the disastrous mess for my missing sneaker. The winding route would be cluttered again once I returned from work, same as always. And same as always, anytime something of mine went missing, it didn't magically reappear.

Not that I took time to dig through the piles of trash close to my five-foot and a couple inches height. When I'd become old enough to realize we didn't live like normal people, I'd attempted to keep the house clean. I got my ass handed to me time and again for throwing out their precious things—stinking, filthy trash.

Sick. Absolute filth. And the stench?

I shook my head, lips pursed.

The little yapper blinked sleepily from atop Mom's lap and jumped down, the tiny bell on her collar twinkling as she pranced after me. At least the little bitch kept quiet in the morning. I let her out the kitchen's door into the back yard. Not that she'd find a nice bit of grass to relieve herself around Dad's shit littering our acre of land.

Coffee pot warming to life, I returned to my room, shoved my feet into my winter boots, and grabbed my cash envelope. My old sneakers' soles had worn out over the previous two years.

"It's time for something new anyway," I muttered to myself, weaving me way back toward the kitchen as both parents continued to snore.

Usually, spring and its warmer weather and rain brought a sense of refreshment and life. I'd yet to experience the vitality that helped keep my spirits from dipping to the point I wondered if medication might be the only way to dig me out of the winter months' depression.

My travel mug I'd cleaned and left on a clean paper

towel for my morning's coffee had disappeared, too, I noted once I let the yapper back in.

More curses muttered in my head as I pulled out the milk from the fridge, and not for the first time, the desire to get out on my own, escape the shit hole I'd been raised in, swelled inside me, stinging my eyes with the need to spill tears down my cheeks.

But tears would wash away the cheap mascara I'd worn that morning.

Spring meant those living off-grid made their way to town for supplies after the long winter. Spring meant Callan Kelly might come calling again—thus the bit of makeup and need to feel somewhat cute. As cute as a waif-thin upper body with thick thighs redhead could be.

While no thrill of attraction spirited my heart away whenever I thought of Callan, warmth of the friendly sort came in to ease the missing sneaker and mug issue ruling my morning.

I'd first met Callan the spring before when he'd flown into town by way of Midnight Sun Charter. A client of Jessie Blacke's, Callan had been all smiles and flirting words. The fact gray hairs peeked through his darker strands above his temples didn't bother me. The age lines around his eyes and mouth were merely evidence of hard years in the wilderness. Hard *working* years. Something neither of my parents could possibly fathom, something I thoroughly appreciated in a man.

He hadn't brought butterflies to flight in my belly or warmth between my thighs, but his character I'd come to know over a summer of sporadic visits had intrigued me to the point I hoped to see him again.

If I were to ever marry a man, he would be the type I would tie myself to. Solid and steady. A worker who didn't shirk from dangers or the challenges of living a flight away from civilization.

In the fall, before disappearing for the long winter, he promised to see me in spring.

Once the snow had started to melt, I'd pulled out that old mascara wand and kept it in my purse. Just in case.

It'd been two weeks since I'd started to see a few of the off-grid families coming in for society and supplies, and while I should have been thrilled to have something to look forward to, I couldn't rouse my emotions past flat.

Bland.

Bored.

Downright depressed.

My eyes stung again as I slipped outside, keys to Dad's old truck in one hand, chipped mug of coffee in the other.

Peeks of sun hinted through the clouds, and I filled my lungs, reminding myself I lived. My heart beat inside my chest. I had my health, even if Mom and Dad didn't have theirs. But those truths didn't lighten the heaviness in my chest, either.

Something new...

Something more than mere sneakers, too.

2

SAIGE

The cashier in the line beside mine did nothing but talk. Chatter, chatter, chatter, complain, complain, complain. She also filled the air with cloying, cheap perfume.

"Ellie had me up three times last night," she grumbled. "Three. And the second time, she woke up Eli. He screamed for an hour straight."

I listened because I didn't have much choice, considering our proximity.

"Billy couldn't be bothered, so it fell to me to take care of them. Big surprise. Some days, I kinda wish I never had the twins, you know?" She huffed and crossed her arms under her large breasts, angled my way while waiting for our first customers of the day.

She'd said similar things before, irking me to no end.

I knew what it felt like to be an unwanted child. I also knew what it felt like to wish for a husband and children like she had. A family of my own. People to *call* my own. A man and children to love like I craved to be loved.

My timidity kept me from both.

"Then Ellie was up at five," she continued when I didn't comment. "What two-year-old wakes up for the day at five in the freaking morning? Like, seriously?"

A hungry one? A thirsty one? I wanted to ask if Ellie had a wet diaper.

I shrugged, leaning down to rearrange items beneath my counter.

"And Billy is goddamn useless."

Fighting against the need to roll my eyes, I bit my tongue and let her spew out all sorts of shit about her husband, complaining about his getting home at night and sitting in front of the TV while she made dinner, fed the kids, bathed, and put them to bed by herself.

She could always ask for help, I wanted to tell her. Tell *him* she was exhausted rather than her co-workers. Or maybe she didn't communicate, and he just didn't give a shit. Dad was that sort of husband and father.

Finally, a customer came through her line, shutting her up.

Fake smile, chatty and happy—at least she made the customers' experience a pleasant one.

I couldn't remember the last time I'd smiled, let alone sang like a canary before I knew the truth of my life. While hostility never crossed my mind, I did my job with efficiency. Unhurried, yet thorough. Packing bags properly, making sure they weren't too heavy for the elderly or frail.

I'd also given up singing even though sad ballads often ran through my head while I lie in bed wishing for...*more.*

The new girl continued to gab as I rang up my first customer, taking care as usual. Initiating conversation didn't come easy for me, so I kept my silence, simply doing my job.

"Have a good day," I quietly stated once handing off the customer's bag, keeping my gaze averted.

"You, too, young lady," the old man said before shuffling away.

Dozens of such transactions a day. Impersonal, but not cold.

Hardly fulfilling, but I got an occasional, "Good job today" from our boss.

The window beyond my co-worker drew my focus in between customers, and an ache spread through my chest as a flock of birds flitted between trees. A breeze rustled the new leaves, and I closed my eyes, imagining it on my face. Fresh air. Quietness. Peace.

"Hello, Saige."

My eyelids popped open at the voice I remembered from the summer before, and my lips actually twitched.

"Callan." No butterflies lit in my stomach, but I didn't mind. I held his gaze all of two seconds before my timidity flitted my attention to the cart he pushed.

"How was your winter, beautiful?"

Heat flushed my cheeks. I started scanning items the second he set them on the belt. "Long. Yours?"

"Longer."

I believed it, living out in the bush like he did. "Survived it, though," I murmured.

"Would it make you smile if I said looking forward to seeing you this spring made it easier?"

Sure that my cheeks blazed enough to cover my freckles, I gulped. No smile, but funny flutters finally woke in my belly.

"I'm in town for the next two weeks," Callan said, setting the last item on the belt. "I'd like to pick up where we left off in the fall—if you're interested."

Pick up...

I glanced up to find his blue eyes serious. Nice eyes, but

guarded and bland, not filled with the heat of passion like the heroes in the tattered paperbacks I got from the library's *free* stack.

Callan had talked me into getting coffee with him the few times he'd been in town the summer before. My first real dates, but he hadn't tried to kiss me. Hadn't held my hand. Hadn't seemed interested other than telling me about his homestead and trying to get me to talk more about my almost non-existent life.

"What do you say?" He smiled, and even though it didn't reach his eyes or warm me between my thighs like my romance novels did, I considered my morning. My depression. My desire for something new. My *need* for such a thing.

Hope pushed to life inside my chest for the second time that day.

A change.

"Same place?" I asked, my voice sounding rusty even though I'd wished good mornings to dozens of people in the previous two hours.

"I was thinking instead of coffee we could get some dinner."

A dinner date. My very first one.

"I-I'd like that," I sputtered, heat once more flooding my face.

"Want to meet over at Dilly's Diner? Say, six?"

My head jerked in a nod as I glanced at the register for his total. "Okay."

Two minutes later, he walked out with his loaded carts, and I caught my attention staying on him far longer than it had the fall before. Broad shoulders beneath his flannel. A bit shy of six feet, dark hair, and beard neatly trimmed.

"You fuck him last fall?"

I jerked my focus across the aisle, my jaw dropping as my co-worker laughed. "N-no!" I sputtered.

"God, you're a virgin?"

That damn heat returned to my face, and I clamped my lips shut, grabbing a bottle of cleaner to wipe down the belt that didn't need it.

"You are, aren't you?" She snorted with laughter. "Girl, you need to get out of your shell and live a little! You're what —eighteen? Nineteen?"

"Twenty-four," I mumbled.

"Shit." She huffed. "I lost mine at thirteen. Hurt like a bitch."

Not a conversation for work... I glanced around to find us alone—for the most part—but that didn't ease my feet shifting in the new sneakers I'd bought myself from aisle thirteen before we'd opened for the day.

"He was hung like a horse and didn't take it easy on me. Your man, there, didn't look the gentle sort, either," she continued running her inappropriate commentary. "Bet he's aching to fuck something other than his fist after a winter out in the wilderness." Another snort. "You aren't much for conversation, but I'll bet after spending that *longer* winter in the middle of nowhere, he'll be more interested in getting his dick wet. Perfect opportunity to give it up if you ask me, Saige. Just sayin'. You're kinda shy, I'm thinking, to lose it on your own merit." At least her voice lowered as a customer approached. "Find everything okay today?" she called to them, all bubbly.

Thoughts swarmed my brain.

A dinner date with a man I wasn't even sexually attracted to.

Something new.

The perfect opportunity.

Was she right about Callan hoping to get between my thighs? Did I want him there?

I hadn't been saving my first time on purpose—I'd just never had the chance to give up the V-card. No boy had shown interest in me during high school, but I hadn't looked up from the floor long enough to see if anyone even glanced my way, either.

Those funny flutters twisted my insides, and I glanced out the window again.

Callan had already gone from the parking lot.

He'd been widowed eight years earlier, he'd told me. Hardly spent any time in town, choosing the wilderness and quiet, instead. He'd spoken of his land, his cabin, as though she'd become his mistress. He trapped and panned a bit for gold to make a living.

No electricity. No running water.

A simplistic way of life that honed a man into something a woman could be proud of. Callan wouldn't get home from trapping and sit on the couch all night watching TV. He wouldn't have pills and beer readily available. From how he'd spoken of his homestead, I knew he treated both with care.

His cabin wouldn't be filled with trash.

He'd become something of a friend the year before— even if I hadn't been the one to fill the silence that sometimes rose between us while sitting down to coffee.

Callan appreciated my quietness, my meekness, he'd claimed. Women, he'd said, oftentimes spoke too much.

I glanced at my co-worker who had her back to me while ringing up Mrs. Dembrook, her chatter a buzz in my ears.

My agreement went with Callan about chatty women— and I looked forward to dinner with more excitement than I'd ever experienced in my life.

3

FLYNN

I caught sight of myself in the still blue of the pool above the waterfall. My bruises had healed in the weeks I'd been in the wilderness, but the pain he'd inflicted inside didn't fade as easily as the outside.

All because I'd fallen back to sleep after he'd gotten me up for the day.

Not like I did it often, but I felt my birthday allowed for a bit of laziness, something I didn't truly understand the meaning of. Growing up off grid from day one out of Ma's womb, I knew the meaning of hard work. Having to take care of the house and Pa when she'd passed, I also knew how to keep one's head above water living off the land.

Pa didn't notice. Didn't fuckin' care how hard his son worked, *strived*, to earn his appreciation and respect.

Finally eighteen, taller and wider in shoulders than Pa, and he still knocked me around. And I stuck around because I'd promised Ma I would. Ten years old, and I'd sworn an oath as she lay there dying that I would look after the bastard who'd hurt her more than loved her.

I'd cursed myself to the equator and back since making that promise, but couldn't bring myself to break it.

Pa was a bastard of the worst sort. Always poking fun, tearing me down, and calling me a pussy if he felt I didn't man-up like I ought to.

Eighteen.

"Time to get the hell out of there," I told my reflection while smoothing down my beard that had begun to fill in. Wasn't the first time I'd said it—wouldn't be the last.

But I had no money. No means of making it on my own. Everything I called mine belonged to Pa, even though I'd helped with the trapping and panning for gold since I could walk alongside him. I knew what those critters felt like ensnared in wire or metal claws—fuckin' *trapped*. Unable to escape. Freedom a long-gone wish. The chance to live ripped from their center like still-warm guts dropping to the snowy ground.

Jaw clenched, I pushed up from sucking down the icy mountain water, swiping my forearm across my mouth.

Eighteen.

Bearded like a man. Seasoned like a man. Officially in the eyes of the law—a man. But I'd never gone to a school. Never drove a vehicle. Never had myself a woman. Never owned a goddamn thing, not even the clothes on my back.

Yes, I wanted to get the hell off Pa's homestead, but where the fuck would I go even if I hadn't promised Ma to stick around? What the fuck could I do? Sure as hell couldn't afford the plane ride into Fairbanks.

Tired of game cooked over an open fire, I trudged down the mountain, feeling as though I had no other choice, my footsteps slow while I forced myself to focus on bathing with real soap in the river. Changing into clean clothes since the ones on my body had crusted over days ago.

Fuckin' filthy animal.

Wildling, Ma had called me when I'd been a kid and she'd been around to show me the meaning of kindness. Always running around half-naked in the summer, my hair long and knotted, scratches and scrapes on my arms and legs. Half-feral, Pa had always grumbled before cursing at me. Made for the wilderness, at one with the woods, wildlife, and Mother Nature.

I'd known nothing but the wilds of Alaska, and I had no wish to know anything beyond. I didn't need to remind myself while standing on a bluff overlooking the greening land stretching alongside the river below.

No smoke rose from the cabin's chimney that I could see from my height. No one moved, either.

He'd be around somewhere, though. Always was—even when I felt sure he didn't watch, catching me doing shit I shouldn't; like skipping rocks across the river rather than tending my fishing pole. Tossing sticks to my dog rather than splitting wood like he'd instructed me to do.

My dog...

The old beagle Pa had brought home from Fairbanks when I'd been eight or so. A dog to hunt with him, man's best friend. Turned out Dog liked Pa about as much as I did, and he'd taken to my side like a summer shadow, tight against my side—ignoring Pa altogether.

He'd tried to protect me against Pa on my birthday, but Pa's fist clobbered him alongside the head, leaving him dazed as me whenever fist or palm met flesh.

But no more.

I straightened and filled my lungs with the mountain's clean air, sucking it in deep until my lungs thought to burst.

"I'm a man," I told Dog, leaning down to scratch beneath his chin. He closed his eyes, his tongue lolling like he was smiling. "Not gonna let Pa hurt either one of us ever again. I'm gonna stand up to him. Won't hurt him because of my promise to Ma, but I'm not going to let him use me like dough Ma used to beat down before making bread."

I stood, my mind set, my feet ready to take me home to begin a new kind of life.

Dog sniffed the air and took off down the path but didn't make so much as a hint of noise from his flapping jaw. Pa had throat-punched him hard enough after his first week of braying pretty much non-stop, that the poor animal couldn't make a sound.

Useless animal in Pa's eyes. A necessity in mine.

Man's best friend—*man*, I reminded myself. I'd tended to Dog ever since. Provided his food, and he kept me warm at night.

Dog continued down the path, flitting glances back at me now and then, making sure I followed his lead, that I would stay true to the promise I'd just made to myself about standing up like the man I'd become.

No sign of Pa around the yard. The cabin sat shut up and quiet, cool, with no evidence of a morning fire—or any recent fire, for that matter.

Hands on hips, I surveyed the two-room cabin, hoping for evidence he'd disappeared in the middle of the day and hadn't been able to return. Dead. Fuckin' gone, leaving me the man of the house.

His neatly made bed sat in view through the opened door into the one bedroom, and the lack of dirty dishes he rarely bothered with, fireplace cleaned out...

He'd gone to town, which meant he'd be back.

"Fuck."

Every part of me wished he wouldn't. If it weren't for Jessie and her bush plane being my lifeline to the outside world, I'd hope his flight nose-dived. Jessie had been lucky enough to survive a plane crash a couple years earlier—and I wouldn't wish it on her again no matter how much my bastard of a father deserved to rot in a shallow grave, feeding worms and bugs in the circle of life.

Jessie had heard Pa give me shit more than once. Seemingly a smart woman, I expected she knew his character. Her kind eyes never failed to catch my gaze, offering me friendship even if we didn't share words privately.

Pa never left us alone.

Maybe he tried to protect Jessie from his wild son, the man who'd never felt the softness of a woman grasping at his dick.

I remembered hearing Pa and Ma in their bed. Kinda hard to not hear as a kid when your parents lay beyond a doorway without a door, rutting away like all animals did. With Ma gone, it'd fallen to Pa to tell me once I'd hit puberty what they'd been doing. He told me all I'd be missing as a teenager and a young man out in the wilds of Alaska.

Teased the shit out of me. Fuckin' relentless in his vivid descriptions of a warm, wet pussy, created just for man's pleasure. What soft breasts felt like in a man's hands. What it felt like to have a woman's ass in your face, slick and ready to suck your dick into her body. Sick bastard wouldn't stop. Laughing after me whenever I walked away to escape the teasing that made me hard as wood.

My focus caught on a pencil drawing that hung forgotten beside his bedroom doorway, pulling my focus off him. I'd fashioned a frame for the image Ma had drawn of me sitting down by the river, fishing pole in my hands, Dog seated next to me. Both of us peered out over the water. The details of our faces made plain what we'd been thinking about...freedom.

At the time, I hadn't realized what I'd longed for. With the wilderness stretching around me, I had more freedom than most. The trap ensnaring me lay in circumstances, and the knowledge no escape was possible kept me down more often than not.

Dog's wet nose touched my hand, and I scratched under his chin again. "You're a good boy," I told him, my throat tightening over the fact I hadn't heard similar words for too damn long.

And I didn't expect to hear them anytime in the near future. Pa would return, and life would go back to shit, until he took another trip into town.

4

SAIGE

Dinner with Callan wasn't much different than coffee. He chatted, and I offered my two cents if he asked. I didn't expound on my home life he'd already dragged from me the year before. He didn't ask after my parents—and I didn't offer.

Neither noticed when I got home, nor did they care when I went straight to my bedroom without cleaning up my trail through the house like usual.

After a lovely dinner with my friend, bitterness damn near choked me at having to pick my way through trash just to get to the only place I could call my own. Even though I'd had a good time, even smiling a few times, tears soaked my cheeks and pillow as I lay in bed that night.

Callan hadn't kissed me, hadn't even suggested he'd wanted to. Perhaps after the long winter, he needed an ear more than a female body. Not that I had much of one to offer.

"Give it up last night?" My co-worker jumped on me the second she walked in the employees' only door at the store's back the next morning.

I ignored her while hanging up my zipper-down sweatshirt.

"Spill, Saige! Give me something. *Please*." She dragged the word out, begging in the tone of the two-year-old twins she always complained about.

"We just had dinner," I gave her, smoothing out the wrinkles of my work shirt.

"Seriously? There's no way I read that man wrong!"

Internally, I begged to differ, but kept my mouth shut.

Callan showed up with flowers an hour later.

Once again, he brought heat to my face, and I agreed to have dinner with him that night.

The relentless woman beside me tittered and teased me all damn day.

Another dinner, another lack of conversation on my part, and another parting with no attempt of a kiss goodnight.

Just friends, I insisted after her relentless questions the morning following dinner date number two.

Two days later, I agreed to a third—one much less expensive than dining out. We met at seven at the coffee shop and ended up sitting on a park bench. An hour in, Callan asked if he could hold my hand.

My palm sweated, but he didn't complain.

"It gets lonely out there."

"I can imagine," I murmured, once more watching birds enjoy their freedom, my insides all kinds of twisted over his palm clasping mine. The first man to hold my hand—the first bit of affection I'd had in longer than I could remember.

My heart might have melted just a bit.

"Thought all winter long about how nice it would be to have a woman on the homestead," Callan said, drawing me out of my own head.

My heart did a funny flip-thing, and I shifted on the bench.

"Saige."

"Hmm?" I forced myself to glance his way but couldn't hold his gaze for more than the usual two or so seconds and ended up watching my free hand pick absently at the frayed edge of my sweatshirt.

"I want you to come back to the homestead with me."

My heart and lungs stalled out. No hint of joking rested in his eyes when my head swung his way. "Wh-what?"

"I want you to come back to the homestead with me." Again, no heat of passion, just a bland suggestion. Even if it made my heart race for some strange reason.

I licked my lower lip, trying to work some moisture into my suddenly dry mouth. "Why?"

"Because I'm a lonely man, and you're a beautiful girl. Kind and quiet." Callan brushed back a bit of hair that had escaped my long braid dangling down my back.

No words of love, no tingles over my body at the touch of his fingertips—not that I'd expected true life to be like the books I buried myself in every night.

I'd been hoping for something new, a change, but...

"I'll marry you if that's what it'll take, Saige," he pushed. "I'm not one for sweet words, as I'm sure you've figured out, but I'm a hard-working man. I know how to see to a woman's needs."

I stared, still unsure what to say.

"You would be a great asset on the homestead, a good helpmate to me," he swayed, his gaze steady and holding mine by the urgency in his tone. "I need a woman by my side again, Saige, and you're damn near perfect."

My throat tightened at the need in his words. It would

force Mom and Dad to get a life—or lose their house, like had been threatened before I'd been old enough to work and support them. They would finally realize what an *asset* I'd been to them rather than the burden they had always claimed.

The coldness they'd shown me my entire life crept in, shutting down any emotion I thought I held toward them outside anger and bitterness.

"Okay," I answered Callan—easy and sure, ready for a new life. One beside a man who would at least appreciate me. Work alongside me in life, and hopefully give me the children I longed for, the ones I wanted to shower with words of appreciation and affection.

His beard twitched as though he smiled, and I quickly went back to my frayed hem, taking comfort in the fact he squeezed my fingers.

———

I had nothing to compare Callan to, so I couldn't say he was hung like a horse, but his thrusting between my thighs while I kneeled in front of him hurt like hell. He'd been rougher than I'd expected, slamming into me from behind until groaning his release.

There'd been no cuddling afterward, no vows of undying love and whispers late into our wedding night, but he'd slept with his hand on my thigh in a possessive hold. And in the morning, his arms wrapped around me from behind, and he took me with less force, the few thrusts it took him to spill his seed less invasive than the night before. Not that I enjoyed it in the least.

Red stained the sheets of the motel room he'd been staying in while in town, and guilt and embarrassment heated my face when we packed up later that morning to fly back to his cabin.

Our wedding had been a rushed affair, a simple "I do" before a judge down at the courthouse a mere week after I'd agreed to marry Callan.

My parents hadn't shown up, but after the screaming and verbal abuse I'd endured after telling them of my plans to marry, I hadn't expected them to be present. I hadn't wanted them there, anyway. My father hadn't ever made me feel like I was more than a nuisance, so I had no wish for him to give me away, nor did I feel he had the right.

I'd packed up my best clothes, a dozen novels, spent all my cash and my last paycheck on a new winter coat, gloves, and boots I would need to survive out in the wilderness. I'd also bought a large supply of feminine pads, hoping I wouldn't have need for them in the months to come.

Callan hadn't touched me before our wedding night, earning my respect, and even though I ached in the worst way possible from having him inside my body, I'd found hope. I'd found my escape and knew that our sex life would eventually get better once I adjusted.

The packed bush plane took to the skies, and giddiness at finally flying like a bird plastered a rare smile on my lips. Add in the three chickens and six chicks in the crate behind my seat, and I couldn't contain my happiness, the emotion rising to hum from my lips in quiet song.

Freedom.

My own home. A big garden, Callan had told me, for which I'd bought a how-to book. A new chicken coop he'd prepared before Midnight Sun Charter had flown him into town. Boxes of canned goods. Staples for the summer months.

A new life, one where my joy of singing in childhood might return fully.

I held onto hope things would get better sex-wise. And until then, I would graciously accept the only way of showing me affection he'd initiated in our time together. If lucky, my belly would begin to swell before summer's end. If doubly blessed, we would fall in love like the couples in my books and live happily ever after.

"Sure you know what you're getting into?" Jessie's voice came through the headphones she'd given us before take-off.

Callan's beard twitched as though her question annoyed him, but he didn't glance her way or turn to face me where I sat behind Jessie.

"Yes," I answered clearly, even though I didn't have much of a clue what I was getting myself into besides what Callan had told me.

"It's not an easy life, but it can be rewarding," Jessie said, banking northward, roiling my stomach as land filled the far window.

I didn't reply, and Jessie went quiet rather than attempt to pull Callan into conversation. Forty minutes or so out, and she spoke again, questioning my husband about the late summer delivery they'd already scheduled.

"You need anything else, just radio it in," she told him. "Same goes for you, Saige."

"Mrs. Kelly," Callan corrected her with a snippy tone even though Jessie and I had been on a first-name basis since I'd started working at the supply store she frequented to fill orders for her clients.

"Of course," she stated without bite, without a hint of the sass I'd heard her husband joke about a few times I'd seen them around town.

Brock always had her tucked against his side, his fingers grasping her hip, his lips finding her hair.

I'd seen them outside the coffee shop once, her arms around his neck, their mouths plastered together. A fairy tale love, the kind I'd thought could only be found in books—one they'd found out in the wilderness, she'd once told me.

I glanced up at Callan, only able to see a hint of his profile from his seat beside Jessie. He stared straight ahead as though focused on the summer ahead, the work that needed accomplished before the warmer months ended.

Perhaps in time, we *would* come to love one another like that. I hoped he would make love to me face to face, giving us the opportunity to kiss. Connect beyond the physical. Thinking on that hope kept my depression at bay—and my smile stayed firmly in place. I even hummed twice more before arriving at my new home.

5

FLYNN

I enjoyed a couple days of peace and quiet. Slept later than usual. Drank a full pot of coffee before doing a single chore. Eating the last can of peaches from the dwindling winter stock set a grin in place that lasted the whole day.

Dog enjoyed the last of the bacon with me, licking his chops, and begging for more.

I let him have the grease, and hell, did I pay for that mistake. His rancid gas kept me up that night, but at least I laughed while grumbling at him.

We sat by the river, and I tossed rocks rather than pan or pay attention to the pole sitting alongside me. The fish I caught, I cooked over an open fire right there by the river. Dog enjoyed the fish guts while I basked in the sun, relaxed as hell and loving life.

A lone wolf came sniffing around, something I'd only seen once in my years on the homestead. Dog and I staked out on the hillside opposite of where his tracks showed him coming down into our valley the day before.

I left out the last bit of grease Dog hadn't lapped up—and that fuckin' wolf came sniffing around again, clear as day in my rifle's scope. Dropping him with one bullet should have been easy, but I'd always been a better tracker than shooter.

He stumbled in my scope as the rifle boomed, jerking my shoulder back, but he still managed to spin and head back the way he'd come.

"Let's go track him down, Dog."

My friend trotted alongside me like I'd trained him to do rather than take off after our prey as his breed were known to do—the same reason Pa had brought him to the homestead.

Dog stayed fixed at my side as I followed the wolf tracks leading up into the hills. Always keeping my head up, keeping an eye on possible routes he might take. Noting disturbed leaf litter. Broken branches. Slight impressions in softer ground.

I had no doubt I would find him. Tracking came easy, but growing up in the wilderness, one had time on their hands, and I'd used mine to get to know Mother Earth and her land. Her creatures. Their signs of passing through.

We found the wolf, already dead and glassy-eyed, a half-mile or so away from home.

I made quick work of skinning him, cutting out his brains for later, and allowed Dog to feast on his entrails before we headed home. Maybe the unexpected wolf pelt would please Pa.

Wishful thinking.

Knowing Pa would attempt to hand my ass to me if I didn't accomplish something beyond a randomly staked-out and brain-smeared skin, I finally set to work on the pile of logs he and I had carried back to the cabin and cut to length the week before I'd taken off.

Having accomplished something before his return might help lessen the verbal blows that usually came after I came crawling back from the wilderness from needing alone time. Confident in keeping my promise to myself and Dog about not putting up with physical abuse any longer, I didn't fear his fists. Since surpassing Pa's six-foot height the summer before, I should have stood up before that last time he'd battered up my face. While his fists *would* stop, I didn't expect he'd ever let up on the shit from his mouth he felt the need to toss my way, though.

Fuckin' prick.

I swung the newly sharpened axe, cleaving a log clear in two, my forehead dented in a scowl at thoughts of Pa coming back and ruining the heaven I'd been living since returning to the homestead. My anger kindled, and I took it out on the dried pine, every thunk a satisfying sound to my ears.

Dog lounged a bit aways, napping in the sun, ignoring me as I tossed the split pieces atop the firewood pile beside him.

"Lazy bastard," I said, my brow smoothing out. My only faithful friend. My confidant. "Dog."

His ear didn't twitch, but the steady rise and fall of his chest let me know he lived.

"Goin' deaf on me, buddy?"

A buzz I hadn't heard since the fall before reached my ears, breaking the peaceful silence around us, jerking Dog's head up off the ground.

"You hear that but not my voice, huh?"

His head swiveled eastward, and I turned as well.

A dot in the sky slowly turned into a plane, its floats and blue logo one I recognized.

Jessie.

My lips twitched into something like a smile before I remembered Pa returned with her.

"Ready for hell?" I muttered to Dog, slamming the axe into one final log.

Dog watched the plane behind me but didn't move other than to lift his nose and sniff.

"Yeah, that's shit you smell—in the form of Pa." I grabbed my shirt, tugged it over my sweating upper body, and carried the axe to the woodshed. Supplies packed the plane, and I would be the one to cart them up to the cabin. I knew I wouldn't be getting back to the splitting anytime soon.

I took my time cleaning up the shed a bit, not heading back into the sun until the plane buzzed overhead.

Brow furrowing over the fact Jessie did a fly by, I stood, hands on hips, and watched her set down on the river a ways off.

"Let's go, Dog." I started down the path toward the river, mouth watering for more canned peaches, but my stomach hard with knowing who came along with the sure case or two of canned fruit included with the supplies.

Dog finally got up off his lazy ass and took off down the path in a lope, tongue wagging, paws kicking up pebbles.

"Run along and get your Scooby snack," I muttered to him, jealous of the affection Jessie would show him and the treats she'd always pull from her pocket after tying up her plane.

While I wouldn't get my hair ruffled or belly rubbed, I hoped Brock had come along and had an extra Snickers candy bar like last time they'd flown in together back in the fall.

Best damn thing I'd ever tasted.

Highly doubting Pa had bought me a couple like I'd asked for the next time he went to town, I followed along after Dog, kicking at rocks as I went. Not so manly an action, but I couldn't find it in myself to care.

6

——————

SAIGE

The cabin and its outbuildings didn't look like much from the air as Jessie took us overhead, but it would be mine. Mine and Callan's.

Ours.

I glanced up to find his profile still bland, hardly interested in turning around to see or ask me what I thought of my new home. Not so much as a glance my way as Jessie landed, the floats dragging in the river's water enough I grasped her seat in front of me, my heart flying near out of my chest.

"Bit bumpy," she said in the earphones. "Sorry about that."

I gulped and nodded, not having expected such a jar for landing in water. Not that I had any landing to compare it to. The flight to the homestead had been my first time in a plane.

The freedom of the skies had been liberating beyond anything I'd experienced, and even though Callan hadn't said two words to me, acting as though I didn't exist on the back seat, I took comfort in what awaited.

Freedom.

No bitter parents to support.

Planting my first garden.

Settling the chickens into their new home—and naming each and every one.

Settling *myself* into the cabin and making my first pot of coffee for my new husband in the morning.

And maybe someday, a swollen belly with a tiny heartbeat snuggled inside.

No butterflies lit with wings in my stomach, but definite excitement tipped my lips upward.

Jessie pulled in to dock, and I struggled to unlatch my seatbelt as she and Callan climbed out.

"Hey, Flynn! Hey, Dog! Want a Scooby snack?"

I jerked my head up at Jessie's raised voice to find her waving at someone.

Leaning forward, I caught sight of a man moving down a worn path through waving grass toward the river, an old dog trotting ahead of him, tongue hanging out in a cute way.

Reddish brown hair pulled back into a ponytail at the man's nape, his short beard a lighter auburn. Wide shoulders filled out a green flannel that appeared much too small for his tall frame. Old work pants, worn boots...

Another wilderness man. Neighbor, I assumed, tearing my focus off his steady gait as he drew closer, revealing him to be closer to my age than Callan's.

A handsome neighbor, too, I couldn't help but note.

My smile faded as a weird feeling moved through my chest, settling like a rock in my stomach. Brow furrowed, I hopped out of the plane onto the dock and busied myself gathering a few personal items from the floor of the plane, my back to the others.

Murmurs reached my ears as Jessie and the neighbor

exchanged pleasantries. Callan didn't speak a word, and every hair raised on my nape beneath the long braid swinging down my back.

Sucking oxygen into my lungs didn't lessen the weighty feeling in my stomach, but I forced myself to turn, two bags in my hands, and move off the deck onto the shore. Focus on where I walked as usual, I stopped once Callan's feet appeared in my periphery.

"Flynn," he said with laughter in his voice, something I'd never heard.

I jerked my focus to his face.

Callan smirked at the man, but no jollity lit his eyes. If anything, he appeared angry, a contradiction to his smile. "I brought you a gift for your birthday," he said and grasped my elbow, yanking me close.

A squeak flew past my lips. My brow furrowed over his words, and I stared at his profile, baffled.

"Callan..." Jessie's voice filled with warning from his other side. She glared at my husband, lips pursed while straightening from feeding the dog a snack.

I dared a peek at Flynn. Eyes, green as dew-kissed moss, peered at me without a hint of emotion, bland as Callan's had been throughout our flight.

My husband let out a dry chuckle. "Brought you a woman, son."

Son.

"What?" I gasped out, the single word ripped from my throat.

Flynn didn't twitch a muscle at the announcement, nor did he take his focus off his...father's face.

Callan tossed back his head and laughed like a mad man, squeezing me tight against his hard body. "Fuck, Flynn!" He barked another laugh. "You should see your face right now."

Flynn still looked as unmoved as he had two seconds earlier. No emotion showed on his face—he definitely inherited that ability from Callan. His father. My husband had a son and hadn't felt the need to tell me.

"Saige here is my wife," Callan continued.

Jessie cursed under her breath and stalked off toward the plane.

"*My* wife," Callan repeated, his voice dropping as Jessie's boots stomped on the wooden dock. Coldness gleamed in his eyes as he peered at his son, his tight hold on my arm starting to hurt. "Maybe I'll share."

My heart stalled out, and I clamped my eyes shut, my mind buzzing, yet unable to form a single thought.

"Just kidding." Another dry, barked laugh from Callan left my insides trembling, and I bit the inside of my lip to keep from making a peep.

His voice, his words, and actions, didn't match with the man I'd known for over a year. He almost sounded... unhinged in his horrid teasing.

I dared another peek Flynn's way.

He didn't speak, and his eyes didn't leave his father to glance down at me. "Welcome, Saige," he murmured, his deep voice hitting me low, bringing back that strange feeling in my stomach.

"Faggot," Callan muttered along with a curse.

Again, no emotion or reaction showed on Flynn's face.

"Go on and get unloading that plane," Callan told him. "Light's wasting away."

Flynn turned and moved off without responding to his father's suggestion he was a faggot or that daylight wasted at midmorning.

My gaze trailed after him as he strode toward Jessie and the plane. The dog followed on his heels.

"You never mentioned having a son." My voice squeaked again, and I forced my attention on the cabin up the path rather than look my husband in the face in an attempt to see what he might be thinking or feeling. God knew my insides were already too troubled to see something beyond a wall shutting me out emotionally.

"Lazy little fucker." Callan grunted and spit, finally releasing my arm from his tight grip. "Go put your shit in the cabin and come back to help upload the rest. It's gonna take a couple hours to get all this stuff sorted."

Cold, dismissive tone—something else I hadn't heard from Callan before that moment. I hurried away, my knees knocking, and breaths coming in short bursts as I wondered what had come over the man I'd married. And what I'd gotten myself into.

Callan had a son. A grown man who did funny things to my insides, even if Flynn didn't refute his father's gay claim. Not that I cared about the young man's sexual orientation. Happiness didn't come easily. People should be allowed to grow in love, no matter where it could be found.

What else hadn't Callan told me? And why had he been so mean in teasing his son? He'd never been anything but kind toward me...

The surrounding wilderness went unnoticed as my mind slogged through turmoil and question. Throat tight, I pushed in the cabin door, breathing in the scent of coffee and wood smoke.

Nothing littered the floor, and only a bowl and mug sat beside a bucket on the built-in shelf on my right.

Setting my stuff down on the small table on the opposite

side of the cabin, I glanced out the window toward the river rather than take in the small but thankfully tidy cabin.

Jessie had crawled into the back of the plane and handed out boxes to Callan and Flynn. He'd called his son a lazy fucker, but Flynn stacked three cases in his arms as compared to Callan's one. Both strode up toward the cabin, and I hurried back outside and toward the river to help as Callan commanded, watching my step, skirting to the path's side as their footfalls approached.

Neither spoke in passing, and I hurried down to the dock without a word or even flitting my attention up toward either of them to make eye contact.

I grabbed the box Jessie handed to me, but she didn't let go.

"Saige?"

"Hmm?" I lifted my head to meet her steady gaze, my palms growing damp against the cardboard.

She peered at me with concern in her eyes. "He didn't tell you about Flynn, did he?"

I glanced up the river to the mountains beyond. "No," I whispered.

"Has Callan ever...been unkind to you? Like, physically?"

I shook my head, too embarrassed to admit I didn't know him all that well, that we had spent little time together, and she released the box.

"Saige."

I forced myself to look her full in the face again before turning away.

"I can take you back with me if you want. You don't have to stay out here with these two men."

While my stomach continued on with its quivering, I wasn't about to be scared into running. Callan and I had married. I'd said I do. Promised to be the partner he needed until death parted us.

Sure, he'd shown a strange side of himself since arriving at the homestead, but hope wouldn't so easily be ripped from my chest.

"I-I'm good."

Lips pursed, Jessie nodded at my whisper. "That changes," she said as I turned, "you use that old radio of Callan's to call me, okay?"

"It won't change," I told her over my shoulder, and set my sights once more on my new home.

New life. No way in hell it could be worse than what I'd left behind.

"What did Jessie say to you?" Callan asked when I walked into the cabin.

I set the box down on the floor and brushed my hands off. The need to lie rose unexpectedly, heating my face. Keeping my focus on the floor, I muttered something about her offering best wishes for my marriage and new life.

He snorted. "Sure she did."

I started for the door.

"You stay in here. Unpack. Canned goods go on the shelving there."

Nodding, I bent to rip open the box I'd carried up. Guess he didn't believe me—and didn't want me talking with Jessie anymore. Did he fear my leaving him? He'd never shown an ounce of insecurity, but again, I didn't know the man that well.

With time, he would see that I took my vows seriously, that I would be the helpmate he needed, the woman I *wanted* to be.

Callan left me to my work, the instant he walked out of the cabin, my shoulders and stomach relaxing.

Pink stained Flynn's cheeks when he walked into the cabin seconds later, boxes in his arms.

"He shouldn't have teased you like that," I whispered to Flynn, watching Callan through the window as he strode back down the path. Turning, I found Flynn openly staring at me—without the shielded gaze from earlier.

"Why are you being kind to me?" he asked, his low voice caressing over my skin even though distrust shone back at me from his vivid green eyes.

I licked my lower lip, trying to rouse some saliva to my suddenly dry mouth. "Because it's the right thing to do."

He held my stare long enough shivers licked over me, pebbling my skin with goose bumps, before he took me in from head to toe and back up again.

His gaze lingered between my thighs.

On my hardened nipples.

On my lips.

My heart thundered in my ears, and I swallowed a rush of saliva as desire, bright and hot, burned in his eyes when they raised to mine. Flutters rushed through my chest, too pleasant, too life-instilling, to be healthy.

Ensnared, I stared back, the tension between us rising to a combustible level. Rippling energy, the kind that flared into flames and burned everything in its path, leaving devastation behind, swelled in the space between us.

"Flynn..." I whispered, not sure what I meant to say, what I *wanted*, or ought to say.

Like a metal door slamming shut, the emotion cut off, emptying his eyes of all life. He pivoted without a word and walked out, leaving me struggling to fill my lungs. Being able to shut down like that wasn't human, wasn't normal. Had I tied myself to a madman whose son behaved just like him?

Callan hadn't ever looked at me like Flynn did, though. Not once did I feel like a double-dipped ice cream cone on a hot summer day.

Shivers licked down my spine.

Arms wrapped around my center, I asked myself again what I had gotten into.

7

FLYNN

"How are you doing, Flynn?" Jessie asked me once Pa started up the path, actually leaving us alone for the first time. Guess he was eager to get back to his wife.

A wife. He hadn't even hinted about bringing one home with him.

Saige's reddish-blond hair escaped her long braid around her face...big brown eyes full of depth and emotion... She'd brought so much need into my body and heart, that I didn't know how to handle myself. I got caught staring before I reminded myself she wasn't mine for the taking.

An ache spread through my groin, and I grimaced. "I'm alright, I guess."

"Did you know about Saige?"

"No, ma'am," I muttered through clenched teeth, fighting off my need to bury my dick in something other than my fist.

Jessie pulled the last of the supplies from the back of the plane and handed them to me. "If you ever want to get out of here, see something beyond these hills, just let me know, okay?"

"I don't have any money. No means of supporting myself," I muttered two of the things in my life I had no idea how to change.

She grasped my forearm, her touch soft as feathers, glancing up at the cabin as though checking to make sure Pa wasn't close enough to hear. "Brock and I have a spare room at our house in town," she said, studying my eyes. "I'm sure we could find you work somewhere."

A shot of adrenaline straightened me at the thought of getting out on my own, but I loved the wilderness. Couldn't leave Ma behind, even if only her bones rested in a grave I'd dug at Pa's orders all those years ago.

I'd made a promise—and I would die to see it through in Ma's honor.

I also didn't trust easily, knowing kindness tended to be used as a lie to get my defenses lowered. Pain of some sort usually followed.

"Appreciate the offer," I said, "but this is my home."

"Callan said you take off for weeks at a time."

"I do."

"Tracking?"

My lips twitch as I consider my favorite pastime. "Anything and everything. Love reading sign."

"So you've said." Her smile warms me like Ma's used to. "You need a place to stay—any time you need some space from your father and his new wife—you head on south to Brock's cabin, okay? It sits empty a lot. I'm sure he wouldn't mind your crashing there for a time if you need to."

Brock's homestead lay a couple days' hike down along the river. I'd only been there once, but seeing as how it hugged the river like Pa's land, it'd be easy enough to find again.

"Appreciate it," I said with a nod, sure manipulation laid beneath the surface of her words someway, somehow, so I kept my initial flare of excitement to myself. "But I'm sure I'll be sticking around most of the summer now that warmer weather is here."

Showing emotion meant giving others a weapon to use against me. Even though Jessie didn't seem the sort, I knew better. Had learned my lesson. Emotions were best left buried, deep enough no one could seek them out and use them against me.

Jessie let out a sigh and released my arm. "Are you still panning for gold?"

"A bit." I hefted the box up onto my shoulder, ready to head up to the cabin before Pa got angry at my lingering too long.

"Any luck?"

"A bit."

"If you ever happen to have a stash of your own, Brock could take care of it for you."

She suggested I steal from Pa—and I didn't cringe at the idea.

"I'll keep it in mind, ma'am," I mumbled, questioning in my head if she wanted to catch me in a devious act—and tell Pa I was a cheating, lying son like he always claimed.

Jessie ruffled my hair, and I clenched my jaw against the sudden tightness in my throat over her display of affection, something I hadn't experienced in far too long. "You do that, kiddo."

I turned, hurrying away, longing for more of her attention that she usually only showed to Dog. Perhaps she was genuine. Perhaps she didn't look for ways to manipulate me.

Perhaps, Saige, too, had meant to be kind rather than find a way to use my thoughts and emotions against me. I'd messed up by allowing her those brief seconds inside my head.

Pa walked my way, Saige tucked in tight against his side, but I continued on toward my destination without glancing their way even though I craved to look into her eyes again. She called to me like a hare to my old dog once more sunning himself by the wood pile—I wanted to salivate and chase after her heels, clamp my mouth onto her neck...

Lips in a thin line, I dropped the box atop the pile outside the cabin.

The fact Pa never took me to town once I'd been old enough to remember more than flashes of color and loud noises meant I'd only remembered two women in my life. Ma and Jessie, and my young heart had been smitten by the sight of the second with her blonde hair and sparkling blue-green eyes even if I didn't trust her.

But Saige...

The third woman in my sheltered life arrived like a burst of flame, lighting my insides like lightning, rushing through me like a forest fire, singeing, burning me to ash.

No longer burdened with a young, fragile heart, I simmered with the lust of a man who'd never touched or tasted a woman. Never rutted between feminine thighs. Never did all those things Pa always teased me about.

For the first time in years, I wished I'd been able to remain Ma's little wildling. Free from responsibility of mind. Free from knowing right and wrong. Free of *want* I shouldn't feel.

Desperation for a mere touch. A brush of my fingertips through Saige's hair hit me like a punch to the gut, but blood rushed southward, swelling my cock to the point of pain, smearing wetness from its tip inside my pants.

No way in hell I could spend the next couple of hours in her and Pa's presence without them knowing what she did to me—even if Pa wrongly thought I preferred men, because I always ran whenever he talked about pussy. Blatantly obvious, my cock pressed tight against its prison, making walking an uncomfortable chore and bringing on the beginnings of a headache from clenching my jaw so damn tight.

Since I'd finished with the unloading of Jessie's plane, I visited the outhouse to take care of that ache. Within three thrusts of my throbbing length through my fist, I shot creamy white from its slit, imagining it coating the insides of warm, feminine flesh. Every spurt ripped a grunt from my chest, but didn't offer relief like it usually did when I took myself in hand.

"Hell," I groaned, clenching my eyes shut as one last shudder rippled over me.

My hand had become well-acquainted with my cock in my eighteen years—but never had I ever imagined a specific woman's face, her touch, while seeking release. Fantasies through the years had been to a faceless body, one with breasts and nipples I could only imagine from Pa's coarse talk.

A warm, *wet* pussy, he'd claimed, the part of a woman that could make a man lose his goddamn mind.

Even a tight, hot asshole would do for a man desperate enough, he'd said just months before. At the time, I'd grimaced, but having sneaked an eyeful of Saige's backside in her jeans...

"Fuck." Tucking my cock back into my pants, I scowled at the evidence of my sick desire.

I'd come over thoughts of Pa's new wife.

She was untouchable.

Off-limits.

What I'd done while thinking about Saige was wrong, but I didn't feel guilt over that fact while tossing a handful of sawdust into the outhouse's hole in the ground.

A part of me wished I'd taken off with Jessie as her plane disappeared into the sky, but beyond not wanting to leave Ma's bones and the vast emptiness around me for a too-loud, too-busy town, I also wasn't about to leave Pa's timid wife alone with him.

I couldn't yet trust her to not dangle kindness in front of me only to rip it away and laugh like Pa always did, but that didn't mean I couldn't look out for her.

Even if he loved her more than Ma, I didn't trust the bastard to keep his hands to himself when he got angry—especially with Saige being a little, defenseless thing. He'd lose his shit with her eventually, and I promised myself I would be there to keep her safe—even if it meant my fist fucked my cock raw to keep from touching her.

———

Night fell, and I tried to sleep with a log wall separating me from Pa and his new wife in his bed. Temptation to change my mind about sticking around churned my guts with the need to puke.

The rhythmic thumps from their room played images through my mind, and every gasp from Saige's plump lips as my father rutted into her rushed that fuckin' need through my balls again. Rustling blankets and feminine whimpers filled my ears. Wet sounds flooded my mouth with drool.

Pa's low grunts from the other side of the wall shouldn't have tightened my sack against my body, but the thought of where he buried his cock time and again, what that softness, that slickened sheath, would feel like wrapped around my own hard length filled me with mind-consuming lust.

I wanted to storm their bedroom, rip him off the tiny woman whose small noises in the beginning hadn't sounded like enjoyment to me. I wanted to take what he did, lose myself in the lust tightening my ball sack.

I realized I stroked myself beneath the blankets.

Cursing under my breath, I dressed in a quiet rush, yanked on my boots, grabbed up my blankets, and crept out into the night, Dog on my heels. I tossed my blankets into the woodshed, stalked toward the outhouse, and once more relieved my lust to images of big brown eyes and flowing reddish-blonde hair she'd brushed out while sitting by the fire in silence an hour or so earlier.

I should have left with Jessie.

Regret lay heavy on my chest, and the night deepened toward morning before I slept like Dog curled up beside me on the hard ground on the woodshed's floor.

8

SAIGE

We had no door to our bedroom. No privacy other than a wall separating our bed from Flynn's. Embarrassment tempted me to put a stop to Callan's attentions once he turned down the lamps, but our situation was my new life. How we lived couldn't easily be changed with the gaping doorway and no lumber mill close by to build up the wall and make a door.

Flynn would be forced to hear his father's grunts.

The thought of the younger man listening to his father take me tingled awareness through my body, dampening my inner walls, easing Callan's thrusts after ten minutes or so of torture. So much for that face-to-face I'd been hoping to bind us together.

Shame heated my cheeks, but I couldn't keep from thinking of Flynn as I held still and let Callan continue to have his way with me. His stoic expression, the stern set of his shoulders, his low, quiet voice when answering direct questions tossed his way from his father over our dinner.

Flynn ignored me entirely, and I wondered over the ache left in my chest because of the inaction. Not once did he meet my gaze after our initial first sharing of words and the heat that had erupted between us.

Not once did he address me, but I also hadn't been able to form words in his presence to even ask him if he wanted seconds of the canned stew and the loaf of white bread Callan had brought from town.

Flynn had packed away the food in silence, and I'd found myself thankful for the supplies that had been stocked on open shelves along the wall and beneath the two beds—the young man would eat us out of house and home.

Unlike Callan, Flynn's lips were full enough to be seen through his beard as he chewed, and even though they hadn't once curved upward hinting at a bit of happiness over my arrival, I couldn't keep that tingling from growing throughout my body while thinking of him as his father continued thrusting behind me.

Wetness swelled between my thighs, and I bit my lip over the sloppy noises his body made pounding into mine, his heavy, hanging balls slapping against my backside.

He didn't groan out sexy words over my wetness, didn't utter a single, dirty thought like the heroes in the tattered paperbacks I'd brought along in one of my bags.

Rather than run his fingertips over my body, seeking out my clit like I fantasized about, he dug them into my thighs, and gave a final grunt while holding me in a bruising grip. Heat erupted against my womb, and I tore my mind off Flynn, praying for a baby of my own instead.

Focusing on the truth of my situation and hoping for the best outcome possible rose prominently in my mind.

Callan pulled out and sprawled onto the bed beside me, leaving me unsatisfied, longing for something...more.

If only I had the nerve to touch myself while he drove into me. Perhaps with time, I would grow more comfortable with our relationship and wouldn't be embarrassed over the thought of pleasuring myself while he found his.

I eased my legs beneath me, stretching out onto my belly, hand clutched between my thighs, and forced my disappointed mind on how the hell I was supposed to clean up the mess coating my palm. We had an outhouse for a bathroom a few dozen yards from the cabin. The chamber pot he'd shown me an hour or so earlier sat beneath the bed's frame, but I hadn't thought to keep a rag nearby.

Callan snored within moments, and didn't stir when I rolled from the bed, hand still keeping his semen inside my body. Fumbling in the dark, I managed to locate one of my socks.

It would have to do.

My throat tightened and eyes burned with unshed tears as I cleaned myself, my husband's snores growing louder—same as the night before, minutes after he'd taken my virginity.

I crawled back into bed, curled on my side, facing the wall, expecting he wouldn't stir or twitch. Same as our wedding night. Would he cradle me from behind in the morning? Rut a bit more gently?

The thought didn't bring back the feelings of need from minutes earlier.

No snores reached me through the wide doorway leading to the rest of the cabin, and I wondered if Flynn slept in silence, or if he still lay awake and staring into the dark, same as me. I wondered if he, too, was thankful his father had finished and lay unmoving except for the rise and fall of his chest, emitting snores enough to raise the dead.

Or maybe I'd gotten lucky, and Flynn hadn't heard.

Wishful thinking, I felt sure.

Forcing my eyelids shut, I let out a steady breath, emptying my lungs.

While I wasn't a God-fearing woman, I believed thinking of someone other than your spouse while in one's marriage bed went against vows spoken before a priest, or in our case, a judge.

I'd committed my life to Callan, to being his wife, his partner, and I'd do best to remember that, no matter how much Flynn drew my eyes and mind. Eighteen, definitely a man, but still my husband's son.

He couldn't be fodder for my fantasies. He couldn't be the face I imagined to ready my body for his father's taking.

My mind stated as much—but my body refused to agree.

The darkness eventually pulled me under, and I dreamed of mossy-green eyes. Soft lips seeking mine. Roughened hands running over my pebbled skin. Desire, hot and wet, coated my thighs, and I let out a moan as he pressed deep inside my body.

Hot breath on my nape. My leg draped over a hard thigh. Fingertips once more bruising my hip—

Callan.

I blinked our bedroom into focus in the morning light, realizing dreaming of his son had made me a sopping mess. At least Callan's length didn't shove into me with stinging pain.

Longing to wiggle away and turn to face my husband, bring us to something *more*, swept over me, but he finished before I found the nerve to do so.

Eyes once more shut in guilt and regret over allowing my timidity to rule me, I lay still after he pulled out and climbed from the bed. No good morning. No kiss on the lips, no smile, or words over our first day together in my new home.

Callan dressed, and silence fell, lifting my eyelids to find if he'd gone. His brow furrowed as he loomed over the bed beside me. "Cook up some of that bacon and eggs we brought along. A batch of pancakes, too."

I pushed to sit, hand once more cradling my leaking core.

He glanced down, but turned and left me alone without sexy words over liking how his cum dripped from me—or offering anything to clean myself with.

Second sock it was.

Throat tight, hating I'd had expectations that set me up for disappointment, I cleaned myself in silence. I also dressed in the corner away from the doorway even though the cabin's front door had shut and I didn't hear anyone else stirring out in the main living area.

Flynn's bed sat empty, I saw when I peeked out into the main living area—but no pillow or blankets remained, either.

I glanced through the front window.

Callan ripped open the woodshed door and looked in. His barked laugh reached my ears through the glass. Face hot, I turned away, not blaming Flynn for escaping the cabin and sleeping elsewhere.

I wish I could have done the same.

"Stop," I whispered to myself, eyeing the cast iron pot hanging above the cold wood stove. "Focus on somehow starting a fire. Make the breakfast your husband requested." *Demanded.* Swallowing, I lifted my chin. "Feed the chickens. Plot out the garden."

Callan had said he needed a helpmate. He needed my help. I would obey his commands to make his food, be the perfect wife, and maybe earn some words of praise.

Determination to be the perfect wife, to earn his respect,

his affection, set me to task with careful vigor. My lips quirked up thinking of a soft hand, caressing fingertips, perhaps a whispered *thank you* against my ear—but I sat in tears before admitting defeat over starting a fire a good fifteen minutes later.

Heart in my throat, I eased open the cabin door and peeked outside. Callan and Flynn had already taken to the pile of wood, axe's swinging.

Flynn had shed his shirt, and my stare snagged on the muscle rippling down his back. Not an ounce of fat clung to his broad frame. Not a single hair like the mat on his father's back. His scraggly ponytail brushed against his sweat-glistened shoulders.

I swallowed a rush of saliva, tearing my attention off him.

Callan stared at me from a few feet beyond his son, axe resting on his shoulder.

"I-I can't—" I cleared my throat, telling my vocal cords to obey as I looked at the ground at my husband's feet. "I can't light the fire," I called out, sounding like a squeaky toddler rather than a grown woman.

My husband let out his dry, barked laugh that I decided I didn't like one bit. A quick glance up showed him shaking his head. He started my way, a frown slowly furrowing his brow.

"You'd better get your act together, Saige," he grumbled as I moved back into the cabin, quickly averting my gaze once more. "Brought you out here for a goddamn reason."

"I-I've never lit a fire before." My response surprised me. Actually gave me a bit of pride in defending myself for a change.

"It's goddamn paper, kindling, and a match." He snipped

the words while crouching down in front of the wood stove, ripping my newfound pride to shreds.

Shoulders slumped, I studied what he did from behind his shoulder and stepped back as the sparks took.

Callan glanced around the kitchen, and I scurried to make it look like I'd done something more toward getting breakfast on the table than shedding tears over kindling I'd stacked all wrong.

My hands shook as I pulled down the coffee container from its shelf. The old-fashioned percolator mocked me, and I swallowed against tears over the fact I didn't know how to make coffee without electricity, either.

"Let me guess—you have no fucking clue what you're doing with that coffee pot."

Guess I'd stood and stared at it too long.

I shook my head, my throat tight.

"Goddamnit, woman." Callan grabbed both items from my hands, and I wrung mine while once more watching and committing to memory his every move so I wouldn't mess up again and disappoint him.

"Think you can at least keep from burning the bacon?" he spat while clunking the pot onto the wood stove's top.

I nodded again, hating that my heart raced, hating that I'd had expectations of rainbows and unicorns once settled into my new life, my new home, with my new husband.

"Speak up, woman."

"Yes," I forced out in a whispered rush, fighting off the sting of tears pressing against my eyelids.

"Shoulda gotten to know you a bit better before dragging your ass out here," Callan muttered while walking toward the front door. "Hope you're better at learning how to live in the wilderness than you are in our bed."

The damn tears slid down my cheeks as I choked back a strangled cry.

"Goddamn frigid—" The rest of his words cut off as he slammed the cabin's door behind him.

Even though tears poured down my cheeks, anger lit bright and strong inside me, lifting my chin and twisting my insides up tight.

So much for words of affirmation on morning one. *Realistic* expectation he would continue in the same vein kept me from agonizing over creating the perfect breakfast.

I burned the bacon—on purpose—because fuck him and his pissy attitude toward someone he'd *known* hadn't even gone camping before. And that comment about my behavior in our bed?

Heat flooded my face beyond that caused by anger.

I set the table, sweat beading on my forehead from working over the hot stove, my hands still shaking. But more from the fact Flynn's presence sucked the oxygen from the cabin as the two of them walked in.

"The fuck is this?" Callan snarled as I set the plate of bacon in front of him. His head jerked up, and his pissed stare singed me before I could look away.

"I burned the bacon," I said, keeping my *fuck you* from my tone, once more pleased with myself for opening my mouth—even though guilt over failing him cringed my shoulders.

"Fucking worthless," he muttered, grabbing up the plate of pancakes I'd browned to perfection—because *I* loved them that way.

I sat between the two men, eyes on my plate even though my racing heart and tight throat probably wouldn't allow me to swallow much of anything. At least I'd had my coffee black and sweet while cooking.

"I like my bacon well-done," Flynn murmured, reaching for the plate.

Tears once more stung my eyes, all anger melting away at his kind words. Something that felt a lot like hopefulness sprang up inside me like a bubbling spring.

"And next I suppose you'll be claiming you like sleeping on the ground in the woodshed rather than in the bed that's been provided for you," Callan said with a snort, dimming my sudden happiness. "Seems my new wife is bringing out sides of you I didn't know about. What else you got fluttering around in that dense brain of yours?"

"Not much, sir." His bland, low tone didn't reveal a hint of reaction to his father's harsh words. I wondered how he could be so callous as to not be affected by his father's words.

Callan huffed a very non-jolly laugh that twisted my insides. "'Course not. Still a faggot or did hearing me fuck my wife make you think about pussy for a change?"

Oh, God. I clenched my eyes shut and focused on breathing, my face hot and heart aching for Callan's son.

Flynn ignored his father with either the patience of a saint or the stubbornness of a mule, and thank goodness Callan didn't push or tease him further.

They ate in silence.

Rock...the only word I could come up with to describe the young man. A good character trait to learn from if Callan continued on with his strange ways and I floundered how to deal with the parts of Callan I'd never seen before.

The sound of silverware against tin plates filled the tense silence, and I managed to get a bite of pancake into my mouth.

My husband's chuckle a few seconds later lifted my head.

He stared at Flynn, his blue eyes cold. "Better not be thinking about touching what don't belong to you," he warned, the threat in his tone unmistakable.

I didn't dare breathe or move.

"No, sir. Never," Flynn said around a mouthful of food, his focus on his plate. "You've made it clear what's yours and what's mine."

"I catch you looking at her like you're wanting to fuck her, and I'll skin you like a goddamn beaver, leaving your entrails as a warm feast for your worthless dog."

"Callan," I gasped his name out on instinct, my insides hot and twisted even though Flynn once again didn't respond with so much as a twitch of an eyelid.

"*You* can keep your mouth shut," Callan said, eyes still hard, and fork pointing my way. "You aren't his mom. Don't have a say over what transpires between me and my faggot boy."

I quickly glanced down at my plate, my stomach threatening to heave back up my coffee and that bite of pancakes I'd browned to perfection.

Flynn's knee brushed against mine, and I barely bit back against the need to quickly fill my lungs. He didn't mutter an apology, and I wondered if he'd meant the slight touch as compassion or apology for his father's unnecessary words.

Either way, that hopefulness once more swelled, but my eyes burned.

I tucked my knees tight together regardless of his reasons and didn't release the tension riding my shoulders until both men once more left me for the outdoors.

9

FLYNN

I shouldn't have been surprised by Pa's behavior at breakfast. The way Saige shuddered beside me throughout the entire meal made me want to punch my fist through his teeth. At least he hadn't gotten physical like he'd done with Ma all those years ago.

Burned food had always earned her a backhand across the face. Weak coffee had once gotten his mug dumped down her chest, and I'd caught sight of her a few hours later caring for the blistered skin beneath her top. My growl at seeing her in pain had gotten me shushed, and I'd promised to let it go.

She'd fallen sick not long after if memory served me right. Not that the burn had anything to do with it. She couldn't get out of bed after a couple weeks and laid there wasting away over the long winter months. Pa refused to radio for help to fly her into town. March came, and still he wouldn't take her to see a doctor even though she'd begged. By the middle of April, she quit asking, and even at ten, I knew her days numbered short.

We buried her up the hill a ways, close to the berry

brambles she'd always collected from once they hung heavy with fruit, her sweet singing keeping the bears under some sort of hypnosis as she'd called it.

The memory of her sweet voice still haunted me. I remembered an old Irish ballad she used to sing me to sleep. Couldn't recall the damn words, but the tune stuck in my head, and when out in the wilds, I sometimes found myself humming it beneath my breath.

Nothing about that first morning with Saige in Pa's home, however, had me bringing the tune to mind.

I helped her with the chicken coop Pa and I had built like a lean-to against the back of the woodshed, finishing up with the chicken wire he'd brought back from town. I'd made the small building bear-proof. We would just need to put the birds away every night, locking them up tight to keep them safe.

Saige held the chicken wire's end as I unrolled it. A quick glance at the cabin showing Pa sitting on the stoop reading a newspaper he'd brought back home.

Seeing as how neither of us had much say in how we'd be spending the foreseeable future, I decided to open my mouth and try my hand at conversation. Get to know her a bit and maybe help ease her way into her new life. Maybe even teach her how to keep Pa from getting to her.

"How long have you known my Pa?" I asked, keeping my voice low enough it wouldn't carry in case my talking to his wife raised his hackles.

"We met last year." Saige glanced over her shoulder and quickly flitted her focus back on the wire in her hands as I snipped it to length. Timid and shy. Unthreatening—and I loved that about her.

"Wishing you hadn't come out here?"

Her head jerked up, a pretty pink blushing her freckled

cheeks. She licked her lower lip, offering me a flash of her cute, crooked front tooth.

My damn cock swelled, pulling my brows into a frown—I looked away from her face before that need from the day before made itself known in my pants and on my face, leaving me vulnerable.

"It's peaceful here," she finally said after too long a hesitation.

"Can be—when Pa's not around," I bit out and pressed my lips tight, hating I'd given her insight to my relationship with Pa so easily.

"Flynn," she chided, but not sounding anywhere near like a mother.

"How old are you?" I asked to steer our conversation away from whatever she might want to ask.

"Twenty-four."

Not much older than myself, still a young woman—and much too young to be wasted on Pa, in my opinion. She'd made a mistake marrying him, no doubt in hell, but her presence, her sweet scent lingering around the homestead made me selfish to the point I was glad she'd chosen to come out to the wilderness with him.

"It's nice having a woman here again," I said, keeping quiet, "but I hope like hell you don't come to regret your decision. Pa can be a real prick."

Again with the slips. What about Saige made speaking my mind so damn easy? What about her made me want to lay myself open to sure manipulation?

"So I noticed," she muttered and quickly clamped her lips shut as though she, too, had said too much.

We tacked up the wire and unrolled another length.

"What'd you do back in town?" I asked.

"Worked at a farm supply store for the past six years."

"Did you enjoy it?"

She shrugged. "It was okay, I guess. Paid the bills."

"Got a family?"

Saige hesitated again before answering. "Dad and Mom, but leaving them wasn't a hardship, I can promise you that."

"Will you miss them?"

She snorted, showing a bit of backbone for the first time since arriving. "Not one bit."

One thing we definitely had in common, but I managed to keep that thought to myself.

We fell silent, and Pa eventually went back to chopping wood.

"What do you do for fun around here, Flynn?"

"Track animals. Follow them deep into the wilds, wishing I could *be* one of them. Been at it so damn long there isn't much I can't follow through the woods and brush. Go hiking. Fishing. Used to draw a bit, but ran out of pencils and paper."

Temptation to complain Pa never allowed for more of either entered my mind, but I clamped my lips shut. I knew better than to let anyone in—I'd also do well to remember that whenever with Saige. She might seem kind, sweet, but...

"Does he hurt you?"

I knew she meant Pa, and while I remembered his fists from the week before he'd gone off to town, I shook my head, not wanting her to worry, not wanting to give her something to use against me. Sure, he'd teased me since returning, but usually, I would have gotten a fist or two within a day of his coming back. Maybe he finally realized I stood taller than him. Maybe he realized I would put up a fight if he tried putting his hands on me again.

"He hasn't for some time," I finally answered, even if my words were a shady bit of truth.

I caught her looking his way a few times, but her pinched expression didn't give me the impression she loved the man—not that I had a clue about such things. Still, if she felt the need for him like my body did for her, I thought sure it'd at least show in her eyes.

It sure fuckin' didn't from what I could see.

Tearing my focus off her face, I cursed myself for a fool, cursed my swelling cock while grasping the lean-to's hatch to let the chickens out from where they'd been stuck all night.

"I-I'm sorry about...disrupting your sleep last night."

Her whisper jerked my head around, our gazes colliding. That pink again...

A muscle ticked in my jaw a few times before I could find my voice since I knew damn well what she referred to. I didn't know how to explain myself—or even what might be considered proper conversation given she'd married my Pa. Not my new Ma, but maybe a friend. Someday, after she proved herself trustworthy. "I've never been in town," is all I could think to say.

For a timid thing, she held my stare as the pink turned brighter. "You've never been with—" Her lips clamped shut, but she seemed to get my meaning.

"A woman?" I filled in for her.

She shrugged and nodded at the same time.

"No. But I'm no faggot," I hastened to add.

"Wouldn't matter to me if you liked men. I think everyone should have the right to love whoever they're drawn to."

If being drawn to someone meant you loved them, my

life was fuckin' over thanks to Pa. I kept that thought, too, from pouring out like water from a barrel.

Chewing on her lower lip, Saige glanced at the door latch I still clasped. While staring at her, I'd forgotten all about letting the chickens out into their enclosed area we'd constructed.

I pulled the door open and stepped into the small, dim interior. The chickens clucked and rushed at my feet.

Saige came in, cooing at the little yellow fluff balls, and squatted to pet their downy feathers I'd checked out the evening before. "Hey, Jessie, Joc, and Jack," she called quietly to the full-sized birds, the black one of which pushed through the chicks toward her.

"You named them?"

"A few of them, yeah. I need to come up with some names for the little ones, though," she murmured, a smile in her voice as the black hen pecked at her hand. "This one is my favorite—Joc. You're such a cute little thing, aren't you?" she cooed at the bird, smoothing back the feathers atop its head.

Saige would have her chickens, her Joc, like I had Dog. Warmth spread through my chest knowing she would have something in our wilderness to find happiness in since hell knew she wouldn't find it with Pa. I couldn't bear the thought of telling her the truth of what cold weather would bring, though.

"Your Pa ought to take you to town next time he goes," she told me, her fingertips returning to trail over the yellow fluff balls skittering around Joc.

I considered the woman close to my knees—on *her* knees. My cock begged to escape. Shove down her throat while I grasped the back of her head to hold her close against my groin.

"Town doesn't interest me," I strangled out, pushing at the thoughts Pa's old teasing over blowjobs brought to vivid life in my head.

Saige peered up at me from where she still crouched, and I shifted away, trying to hide the bulge in my pants. "No friends—no schooling. No women. How can you not want those things?" she asked.

"Ma taught me how to read and write. Pa taught me how to survive out here." I shrugged. "If I ever decide I want a partner in life, Pa says there's mail-order type brides."

Saige choked on a giggle—a beautiful sound if I'd ever heard one, her crooked front tooth just as cute. "Seriously?"

I shrugged again, my lips twitching.

"What if she stinks like rotten onions? What if she's more beast than beauty?"

Would it matter to me as long as I had a partner, I wondered?

A quick glance down over the tiny woman pushing to stand beside me, and I realized Saige had a point. My partial smile flatlined. Having seen perfection, I feared nothing else, no mail-order bride, would be good enough.

Off-limits, untouchable.

I stalked back outside at the self-reminder, leaving the watering and feeding of the chickens to Saige. Time to fuckin' bust another nut, as Pa called it. Empty my balls before I followed after her with my nose up her ass and salivating like a buck after a doe in rut—'cuz she smelled damn delicious.

A forbidden fruit, my temptation. And I feared my downfall.

10

SAIGE

A wareness of Callan's stare slid shivers down my spine as I sprinkled a bit of feed around the newly enclosed pen for my little sweeties—and those I'd yet to name.

Not a good shiver, either.

Dark energy, like tendrils of fear and unease, snaked through my mind, slowing my heart to a heavy thud in my chest, stealing my joy in the cute chickens.

Covert glances around revealed Flynn had disappeared —and Callan studied me from the stoop where he once more sat.

One last sift of feed through my fingertips, and I brushed my hands down my jeans.

"Saige!"

I turned at Callan's call, tucking away thoughts on naming the birds for later.

"I'm hungry!"

Then make yourself a damn sandwich or something.

Teeth clenched, I let myself out of the gate and started toward the house. Focused on where I walked, I couldn't see

Callan's face—but that unpleasant energy swelled through me as I drew closer to where he'd sat.

He grasped my elbow when his boots came into view and pulled me into the house, spinning me around.

My breath left in a rush as he pushed my face against the log wall, his hands grasping at my jeans and yanking them to my ankles. I whimpered at the painful burning over my hips where the material chafed me raw with the harsh, downward swipe.

"Hungry for *pussy*," he said, standing once more behind me, his breath hot on my ear.

What should have been sexy words, the type to make a woman drip with want, dried my mouth. Eyes closed, I bit my lip as he shoved two fingers between my thighs.

"Fuck, woman, you've got one fickle pussy. Dry, then wet, then dry...the fuck is your problem?"

The fingers disappeared. He spit—and his slickened length shoved into me with one grunted thrust, slamming my hip bones into the wall.

A shriek screamed from my lips as pain seared my insides.

"What?" He growled against my ear, sending shivers over my skin. "My cock isn't doing it for you today?" He bucked in again, slamming my hips against the wall a second time as I fought to control my sobs. "I'm not pretty enough? Young enough in the light of day?"

Tears soaked my cheeks as he yanked me backward far enough he could bend me at my waist, his fingertips once more digging into flesh that still felt bruised from the night before.

"I know you think *Flynn* is pretty. Thought sure being close to my son would make you wet," he grunted, plowing into me. "It's why I let you alone with him those few minutes in the coop. Make you enjoy my fucking you."

Still sobbing, I placed my hands against the wall, head hanging. Enduring. *Hardly* enjoying.

Raw and sore, my insides refused to ease his way. I wanted to crumple into a heap on the floor. Sink through the floorboards and disappear into the earth.

Mistake. I'd made a horrible mistake.

And now there's no escape.

"Guess I was wrong about you wanting my son." Another deep thrust and wet heat exploded inside me.

Thank God.

I continued to bite back my sobs and didn't move when Callan pulled out, once more leaving me dripping. His seed splatted on the plank floor—and I let it, uncaring about keeping it inside me to make a baby.

Why would he treat our child better than he did Flynn? I expected he wouldn't, and I couldn't stomach the thought of an unkind father even worse than my own.

"I gotta go take a shit," he announced as though discussing the weather. "It's laundry day. See it gets done."

With that barked order, he left the cabin, leaving me alone.

Sniffing and searching for a backbone, I straightened, and eyed my home as my jeans stayed wrapped around my ankles, Callan's cum sliding down the inside of one thigh.

I didn't want to regret my choice, but my heart felt it all the same. I wanted to hang on to hope that things would get better, even though the dismal reality of my new life settled over me like a black shroud. The memory of my parents' house, regardless of the mess and stench, suddenly didn't seem as horrid as I'd once thought.

My sobs broke free as I cleaned between my thighs, teeth clenched against my stinging, swollen flesh.

Something had to change to make my new life bearable.

I just needed to figure out what and how.

11

FLYNN

Saige seemed to melt inside herself. No words, no hint of a smile. It's like the tree she'd taken life from had frozen up for the winter, dropping her like a dying leaf to the ground.

Pale cheeks. Sad eyes.

My heart ached for her, and I focused on trying to make things better.

I studied the gardening book she'd brought along to the homestead, and we set out together to create life in the fenced-in garden area Pa and I had readied the fall before. We worked side by side, more silent than not, Pa always looking on.

The one time he went to the river to fish for some dinner, I decided to get her to open up. Probe a bit to see how I might make her life bearable—even though just being near her made mine the opposite.

I hadn't fucked my dick raw but was well on the way.

"You're not happy out here," I went with the truth, hoping she would allow herself to be vulnerable with me since she knew Pa treated me the same. That I wasn't prying to manipulate.

She hesitated long enough I thought she hadn't heard me. "My head tells me I made a mistake," she finally whispered, glancing down the pathway leading to the river where Pa had disappeared. "But my heart holds onto hope."

I bit back a Pa-like snort. I hated to be the one to set her straight, but I didn't know how to be much of anything but honest. "He's always been a bastard."

She stared at the soil between us, her brow furrowed and lips working like she lost herself to her thoughts.

Pity for the tiny woman twisted my insides up tight. "Maybe your softer nature will be a good influence on him," I offered, although I didn't hinge any hope on the statement.

Saige continued to stare, the deep groove between her eyebrows sending that tightness in my gut up to my chest.

"You're an incredible cook for someone who never used a wood stove before." I said the first good thing I could think to ease her a bit.

The frown smoothed out.

"I burned his bacon," she muttered, dropping a radish seed into the shallow furrow she'd made with her fingertip.

At least I'd pulled her from her unsettled thoughts.

"The pancakes were perfect," I added, hoping for more of her frown to disappear. "So was the coffee."

A small tilt of her lips swelled lightness in my chest, eased the ache her sadness had brought. I fuckin' loved the feeling. Breathed it in. Soaked in its warmth.

Saige needed encouragement. Words of love—since I couldn't give her anything more.

"You've got a way with those chickens, too. Never seen an animal take to a person so quick since Dog."

The lazy bastard sprawled outside the garden's fence.

"He follows you like a shadow."

I nodded, love for my one friend filling me up even further. "He's a good boy. Loyal. A good hunter—when he's not lazing around."

"Every beast deserves rest on occasion."

"Tell that to Pa," I muttered before thinking I might bring her spirits back down.

Her light chuckle jerked my attention her way. *"Daylight's wasting..."*

My lips twitched at her mocking tone, and she glanced up, her focus snagging on my lips.

Instant heat flared to life, and I cleared my throat, turning my attention on the tiny beet seeds in my palm.

"You ever been out in the wilderness before?" I asked, my tone rough from fighting the swelling in my pants.

"Never."

"Ever gotten close up and personal with big critters? Bears and such?"

"No."

I buried the last beet seed and leaned over the bed, using my fingertip to make prints in the freshly tilled soil.

"What's that?" she asked, leaning closer to watch.

"Bear print." I created another, but smaller, missing claw marks. "This here's a wolf. You see either anywhere near the homestead, you let me know." I sat back, brushing my hands together to rid them of dirt.

Saige nodded and sat back, busying herself with planting radishes again. "You must know a lot about surviving out here in the wilderness."

"It's been my playground," I said, eyeing the sunlight glinting off her reddish-blonde hair. "Never been on a swing or slide-thingy Ma told me about."

A heavy sigh left Saige's shoulders stooped, but she

didn't lift her head to look at me. "You've missed out on a lot, Flynn."

"I wouldn't change it."

That got her attention, and I damn near drowned in her soft gaze. "No?"

Muscle ticking in my jaw, I glanced over the mountains rising behind her. I sure as hell would change a lot about my past. Pa. Losing Ma. But, if allowed to change my past, I wouldn't have gotten to sit and plant a garden with Saige. I wouldn't have gotten the chance to enjoy the peek of her crooked front tooth on occasion. I wouldn't have been able to draw her sweet scent deep into my lungs whenever she passed by me.

"No," I finally grunted my reply, pushing to my feet. But I wouldn't tell her why. Couldn't give her that truth to hold over my head.

"My being here brought you more difficulty, didn't it?" she asked as I turned away.

I paused from walking out of the garden area, taking advantage of my height to note Pa sitting at the river's edge, his back to us. The arrival of his wife had certainly changed things for me, but Pa would have found something else to tease me about had he never met Saige. He didn't need or lack ammunition to be a bastard.

"You're not a burden if that's what you're saying." I turned to find her pushing to her feet, brushing her knees off. "You're a gift, and my father is too much of an asshole to recognize it."

Her eyes latched onto mine, welling wetness over her brown orbs making my arms itch to pull her against my chest.

"Why do you do things for him when you'll only ever fall short?" I voiced the unintended question with ragged words.

She held my stare, her lower lip trembling. "Because I want his attention and love—not to be ignored and just used for his pleasure."

I knew the feeling deep inside my soul. Had since childhood. I craved his edification, attention of the good sort. For too long, I'd striven to be what he wanted, to prove him wrong in his assumptions about me. For too long, I'd believed myself unloveable because of how Pa treated me, but memories of Ma and her affection battled those thoughts.

Saige had mentioned she didn't miss her parents—wouldn't. She ached for the same I did, but she didn't have memories of anyone to assure her she had worth.

"I appreciate you, Saige," I told her, needing her to have something to hold on to whenever Pa got to be too much.

A tear slid down her cheek as she blew out a heavy exhale. "Thank you."

She moved past me, her hand reaching to touch my forearm. Bare skin contact—the first between us.

My dick swelled in a rush, and I stilled, the need to pounce like a predator tensing every damn muscle in my body.

Saige squeezed my arm. "Thank you," she whispered again, peering up at me.

I stared after her as she walked away, my dick leaking, but my heart just as moved. A soft touch. Kind words.

Throat tight, I rubbed at my forearm, hoping to soak the tingles from her gentle caress clear beneath my skin to hold onto forever.

I couldn't have her, told myself to quit thinking about having her, but I couldn't fuckin' stop it no more than I could the rising of the sun or the howling of winter's wind. My body ached for her, and I feared squashing down my brewing want of her would only lead to an explosion neither of us would survive.

12

SAIGE

Callan returned from his fishing expedition with a scowl on his face. I'd learned to pay close attention to his moods, his ever shifting emotions.

The man's mind definitely unhinged at times, going from bland to furious in a blink. I hated his continued suspicion over my wanting Flynn even though I did everything in my power to avoid being alone with his son. I schooled my features the best I could. Kept my mouth shut.

I kept my nose to the grindstone so to speak, doing all he asked, just like Flynn had mentioned. Nothing gained me kind words from my husband like Flynn had so graciously offered. Fighting to keep the moment of happiness he'd given me off my face, I hurried to the house, wanting to escape whatever new shit Callan decided to complain about.

"Where the fuck's lunch?" he spit out, poking his head in the cabin's door seconds later.

It wasn't yet noon, but I didn't mention that fact. "I'll make it now if you're hungry."

"Goddamn right, I'm hungry. Been working all morning long," He slammed the door, leaving me alone.

"Can't read your mind," I muttered quietly, hating how quickly he smashed the lightness I'd felt in my step after Flynn's kindness.

I made my husband and his son lunch. Cold sandwiches —with a nice glob of spit inside Callan's—because once more, fuck him and his pissy attitude. The plates trembled in my hands as I approached them out by the woodpile.

Flynn sat closest to me. "Thanks," he murmured as I handed him one a plate.

"You serve your husband first," Callan barked.

"I'm sorry." I almost dropped his plate as I handed it to him, and I bit my tongue, hating the apology had come out on its own. Steeling my spine, I decided right then I would never again apologize for not knowing how he wanted or needed things.

I would learn from studying his face—I was determined to do so in order to make thing easier.

Sick satisfaction still rose inside me as he tore into the sandwich, swallowing down the little present I'd left him inside the bread.

"Coffee," he ordered.

"What about it?" My mouth let loose before I thought better of it.

Anger flared in Callan's cold eyes at my snipped tone, and I quickly turned my focus to the ground. That backbone swept away like dust in a gust of wind. Even my damn eyes stung. "Get me some," he said, his voice even colder.

I spun, muttering in my head that a *please* would have been nice even though I should have known better. Callan always wanted coffee after a meal.

A few minutes later, I'd stirred the morning's coals in the wood stove to life and set the old fashioned percolator on top. Sniffles still had my nose, but at least the tears had stopped.

The door opened behind me, but warmth spread over my skin rather than the snaking, dark energy Callan always brought.

Flynn.

A sense of urgency tingled my skin, but I found my shoulders relaxing, my brow easing from its frown.

"You okay?" His low voice pebbled my skin. A simple question, a hint of concern, and I needed to fight off the thickness swelling in my throat again.

"Yeah," I whispered, pulling down the two mugs I'd put away after breakfast. "You want some coffee?"

He didn't respond, so I glanced over my shoulder.

Flynn stared at my thick thighs, the desire in his eyes raw. Ravenous.

Heat flushed through me in a rush, bringing with it the wetness Callan coveted.

Thinking of Flynn had made me wet a few times while Callan took me...had made things easier. Wetness again made me ready for a thrusting cock, but with someone I couldn't ever have.

I bit my lower lip as the answer to my problems dinged like a bell in my head. Fantasizing about Flynn while having sex with his father was totally wrong, but would at least make that part of my life a thousand times easier. Perhaps I'd come to enjoy Callan's rough taking if my body climbed aboard the sex train.

"Saige?"

Blinking, I tore my focus off the bulge in Flynn's pants I hadn't realized I'd been staring at. A loud gulp reached my ears as our gazes collided. Heat flooded my face. "I-I'm sorry—"

Flynn turned, shielding me from his obvious arousal. "I hate how Pa speaks to you."

"It is what it is," I rasped, mugs clasped to my chest, knowing he must hate the fact I, too, felt the wrath of his father's twisted mind.

His beard twitched as he washed up his and Callan's plates, his back to me. "I'm sorry for the way he treats you." His bland tone didn't reveal concern, but strangely, I trusted the young man's words, same as I'd done with those he'd spoken over the garden bed.

"It's not your fault."

"I didn't stop him from hurting Ma—but I won't let him hurt you." Flynn turned to face me, a hint of pain in his gaze he quickly shrouded. "Made a promise to her which I've kept, and now I'm making one to you, even if it means trumping hers."

My stomach twisted into a tight knot even though I didn't understand all of what he said. "You need to stay out of it, Flynn. Please. I-I'm afraid of what he'd do if you tried to intervene."

I didn't feel the urge to look away, glance down, or wring my hands—I couldn't look away from the need that once more swelled to fiery life in his green eyes.

"You can't look at me like that," I whispered when he didn't reply.

"Can't help it. I'm a wildling born of the wilderness, Saige. Don't know the first thing about women, fuckin', or relationships. Just know I'm drawn to you like Dog to a hare. Like animal blood lust. Need I don't know how to erase— and don't want to even though it's brewing up like that there coffee pot ready to boil over."

Oh, God. Biting back my whimper, I pressed my thighs together.

Flynn's nostrils flared, and he glanced out the window before turning once more and closing the distance between us.

My breath caught as he loomed over me, hands fisted at his sides, mere inches separating us.

"D-don't," I whispered, even though my hormones screamed for him to do whatever the hell he wanted with me.

His jaw twitched beneath his beard. "If he ever hurts you like he did to Ma, like he did the other day I heard you sobbing... I'll kill him."

The other day.

My face paled as I realized he must have heard his father take me right inside the cabin door. The day he'd hurt me enough I'd had to beg him to let me heal before taking me again.

No anger laced Flynn's words, but I didn't doubt his promise to me or the tension riding his shoulders.

"He won't ever hurt me like that again," I stated, trying for an assured and steady tone.

Flynn studied my eyes. "You gotta know him better by now, so how can you be so sure?"

The truth would shock—and without doubt ruin whatever regard Flynn might have for me, even if he wanted me as badly as I craved him. Lips clamped, I swallowed what I wanted to tell him.

That I would imagine it was *his* hands on me whenever his father took me. *His* hard cock fucking into me. That thinking of *him* would ensure sex with my husband wouldn't hurt.

Wrong. So, so wrong...

Flynn's focus dropped to my lips, catching my breath and stalling out my rapidly thumping heart.

"Flynn—don't."

Footfalls sounded beyond the door, and he spun away, dropping to his knees by his unmade bed as though searching for something beneath it.

I turned and busied myself retrieving the tin of sugar and a spoon with my hands that didn't seem to be able to do anything but shake.

Suffocating heaviness fell over the cabin's interior like a shroud as the door opened, tightening my stomach into the knot I'd come to despise.

Callan didn't speak a word, but the weight of his stare, his damn silent insinuation that something sinful transpired behind his back threatened to bring up the apple I'd eaten while making their sandwiches.

I'd started a new life, one I'd never expected or hoped for.

One I would have to fill with lies in order to survive—emotionally and possibly physically as well.

According to what Flynn had said, Callan had hurt his first wife, but to what extent? Asking would only bring more pain to Flynn, who obviously blamed himself for not stopping his father's abuse of his mom.

The thought I ought to just tell Callan I'd made a mistake, that I didn't belong in the wilderness and wanted to go back home, rose in my head, shooting hope through me like rays of the morning sun.

Sounds of something dragging on the floor from beneath the bed drew me back to the truth of my situation.

Flynn.

Dimming clouds shut that hope right the hell down. I couldn't leave him there alone with his father. Even though

Flynn stood taller than Callan, even though he was no young boy, I felt an instinctive need to protect him.

Leaving would make Callan angry, and I wouldn't be the one responsible for bringing possible harm to Flynn, who would surely reap the consequences of my choice.

I refused to acknowledge that even more so, I didn't want to leave Flynn, that I felt an unearthly, unhealthy need to stay as close to him—so I could continue breathing.

13

FLYNN

I'd wanted to kill Pa for what he'd done to Saige a few days earlier. Small, frail Saige. Beautiful, curvy, woman. She smelled delicious standing there in that kitchen, sweeter than any canned peach, and the dried tear tracks on her cheeks had tempted me to flick out my tongue for a taste, Pa be damned.

But she'd told me not to when I'd stared at her lips, considering what I wanted to do with them.

She didn't want me like I did her, otherwise she wouldn't have told me not to. But what did I know about women and relationships? Nothing—exactly as I'd told her.

I pulled Ma's old easel from beneath my bed frame. I'd only dropped to the floor at the sound of Pa's footsteps in order to throw off his scenting a trail he was right to suspect, but at the dusty sight of the lap desk tucked atop it, my thoughts turned in a circle, leaving thoughts of tasting and taking far from my mind.

Ma.

Lifting the lid while sitting back on my haunches

flooded memories through me. Bits of pencil and old papers stuffed into the bin.

"What are you doing?"

I didn't turn to address Pa's question. "Just wanting to remember," I muttered, lifting the top most picture.

He mumbled something about the light wasting away like usual, but I ignored him, caught up in the scribbled image. The one she'd worked on her last days while lying in her bed.

"What's that?" Saige asked, her voice quiet as clinking noises of mugs and the sugar tin sounded behind me.

"Ma's drawings and supplies."

"Did she draw that one of you and Dog on the wall?"

I nodded, tracing a finger over the shading of the rock she used to sit on up by the brambles—but she'd drawn an image of me sitting there instead. "She used to sit up near the brambles and draw for hours."

"Fucking waste of time, too," Pa grumbled. "It's where you got your damn laziness from. Got that coffee ready, woman?"

Saige murmured an affirmative while I ran fingers over dark lines and softer shading. Why had she drawn me rather than herself? Dog and I hadn't ever sat still like that all those years ago.

Dog rested at my feet in the drawing, one of my hands on his head, the other settled atop the stacked rocks she'd made arm rests out of.

Ma.

Tears clogged my throat, but I swallowed them away. Couldn't give Pa anything to tease me about.

All of three minutes passed of him slurping coffee, my mind reminiscing and throat slowly relaxing, before Pa grumbled to me about getting back to work—because, once again, we wasted sunlight.

The logs wouldn't drag themselves back to the homestead. The wood wouldn't chop itself.

I laid the drawing back down on top of the other papers and left the lap desk on my bed. "You're welcome to look," I told Saige while moving past her to follow Pa outdoors.

"Thank you," she whispered, and I nodded without meeting her gaze that seared my skin until I shut the door behind me.

———

After another week of sleeping in the woodshed, my bones ached, and I figured maybe enough time had passed that Pa wouldn't be fuckin' Saige every night. I moved my blankets and pillow back into the cabin after dinner to Pa's sneering.

Saige stood with her back to me, washing up the dirtied dishes from dinner. In her two weeks on the homestead, she'd mastered starting fires and cooking on the wood stove, just like I'd told her. She'd somehow raised the old sourdough starter that had been ignored for a few days too long back to life, too. We'd had biscuits that night with the last of the butter Pa had brought home from town.

Having had that rich fat to smear on hot biscuits, I decided that someday, I'd have a cow of my own. Maybe three.

I took to drawing on the last of Ma's bit of paper—Jessie's float plane from memory, sailing over the homestead. Something to gift to her when she flew in come September with our winter supplies.

Pa sat on the stoop smoking his pipe, the open door letting in the sweet smoke, taking my memories back to easier years, the pleasant memories that had dimmed due to his getting cranky with age. Not that he'd ever been affectionate or offered kind words, but the fists hadn't come my way until around the time Ma died.

But I refused to think on the non-physically abusive Pa from way back when. It didn't excuse or make his other kinds of abuse any easier to swallow.

Having finished my drawing, and feet itching to move, I went outside and up the hill to sit by Ma's grave. The sky had begun to darken, bringing a cooler bite to the air, and I hunkered down in my flannel, watching Saige slowly make her way to the outhouse and back to the cabin again a few minutes later. Shuffling feet seemed to procrastinate, but hunched shoulders beneath her sweatshirt suggested the cold drove her indoors sooner than she'd have liked.

I'd noticed in the previous week she stayed out as long as possible, enjoying the silence and space Pa allowed. At least she had her books to keep her company. I expected loneliness pulled at the corners of her mouth, lips I tried to keep from staring at. Lips that hardly ever smiled, had never let out a soft giggle like the one that haunted me from our time in the chicken coop.

We'd worked alongside one another readying the rest of the garden, and she spoke about town—the sights, the sounds, the scents—nothing of which she said she missed. I doubted her words, though, for I often saw her staring off into the distance like I did, as though wishing for *more*, some unnamed, elusive thing that would fulfill our sorry lives.

I stayed put until Pa the lamp light in the window winked out. Even then, I waited a full fifteen or so minutes before creeping back down the hill and letting myself into the cabin.

The sounds of wet fucking met my ears, and I held my breath, halfway in the door, my cock springing upward.

Teeth clenched, I went to turn away and wait until Pa finished, but a breathy, feminine moan slid over my skin, tensing every muscle in my body.

My other foot stepped into the cabin.

I shut the door silently behind me.

Another soft moan, a steady thump and what sounded like slapping skin—the kind without pain, the kind I'd never known.

Cock aching, I sank onto my bed facing the wall, imagining Saige's eyes on me, I imagined it being my body causing her to gasp and whimper with pleasure rather than the agony I'd heard before on that afternoon a few days earlier.

My hand stroked over my length as I strained to listen, every rustle of blanket and soft noises leaving her mouth coursing animalistic need through me. Even Pa's grunts couldn't tear me from my fantasy of bringing Saige pleasure. Of touching her skin, kissing and licking. Devouring her like the sweetest, dripping peach.

Pa groaned, and the thumps fell silent.

I squeezed the base of my cock to keep from emptying my balls and groaning my own release Pa and his wife would be sure to hear.

An hour passed before I kicked off my boots and pulled my blankets over my heated body.

Sleep refused to come.

14

SAIGE

The first couple of times I imagined it was Flynn's hands on me rather than Callan's, guilt swamped my mind, fought my body's reaction to the forbidden fantasy. Within a matter of weeks, however, that feeling of doing wrong retreated.

Callan refused to make love to me face to face. He refused to kiss or even touch me outside of our bed. A few times, I'd been turned on by thinking of Flynn and attempted to be affectionate with my husband. And with every avoidance of my timid advances, Callan intensified my regret over choosing to marry him. Every night he passed out after filling me up with his cum before I'd had a chance to climax, and I prayed to God no seed would take.

When my period finally came, I cried happy tears—and enjoyed the five days of respite from his attentions.

Feminine blood, my old hated friend, became my newest and best I never wanted to leave.

Callan still slept like the dead, snoring and unmoving while I lay awake, unsatisfied, and staring in the dark, Flynn quiet on the other side of the wall.

He kept away from me as I'd asked, and Callan eventually stopped with the accusations and teasing. I still felt his suspicious stare whenever Flynn worked alongside me, but I kept everything between us on an absolutely platonic level.

But his heated glances he wasn't able to keep inside sometimes when Callan wasn't looking, and the resulting heat flushing through my body...

Just the scent of him, the wildness and ozone clinging to his clothing, warmed me through to my inner-most parts. Craving didn't begin to describe what I felt toward Flynn and his quiet, gentler nature.

My fingers itched to touch him, offer gentleness he must not have had since childhood. I told myself my longing came from his being denied for so many years, but I knew I lied to myself. I wanted to touch him because *I* wanted it. Needed it.

Flynn had taken to teaching me everything he could think, showing me how he'd built the coop extra strong to protect my little friends from predators. How to read other signs of critters around the homestead—tiny tracks and disturbed areas we never walked on.

The more I learned, the more my confidence grew, but exhaustion from constantly being on guard, striving for perfection over household chores and wifely duties, dragged me down. I pushed onward, determined as ever to make the most out of my new life, pushing all thoughts of Flynn from my mind except for when Callan wanted to fuck me.

Repeated failures of other wifely duties, however, weakened my resolve to keep my vows.

Twice, I'd brewed the coffee too long, and it came out black as midnight and as thick as molasses. I burned another batch of bear "bacon", and not on purpose. The first time I'd attempted all on my own to fry up the newly caught fish Flynn had handed to me, I'd left more flesh stuck to the bottom of the cast iron pan than ended up on the dinner platter.

And it'd been a good, seasoned pan, too.

"The fuck, woman!" Callan cursed a few more times, slamming the pan back onto the wood stove when he noticed what I'd done. "Stupid, fucking woman!"

Flynn stepped through the door, his brow furrowed, quickly taking in my cowering form by the table and his Pa still hunkered over the skillet I'd ruined.

"Burned our dinner," Callan muttered, sitting his ass in his chair like he planned to wait for me to fix my mistake.

"It's my fault, Pa," Flynn stated before I could offer to whip something else up. "I showed her how to fry the fish last time, but I probably forgot to tell her how hot the pan should be."

Callan grumbled a few curses, tossing in lazy and useless while glaring at the both of us.

My insides turned hot, but I bit my tongue. His sweet son, while lying about forgetting to show me the proper heat of the pan, thought to protect me from his father's wrath, and the asshole belittled him.

I wanted to kiss Flynn—and smash that damn skillet over Callan's head.

"I-I'll get something else together," I sputtered out, forcing a smile. "Just be a minute."

Callan glared at me, blue eyes icy enough shivers slid down my spine. "Hurry it up. I'm starving."

Failure after failure ended up following me through the next couple of days, and anytime Flynn happened to be around, he blamed himself.

My heart melted. My chest ached. My damn head felt ripped in two.

Sometimes exhaustion kept me from fantasizing about Flynn while Callan took me, and *those* moments of failure ended with me in tears and pain from torn flesh between my thighs.

But I bit my lip. Kept in my cries, lest Flynn hear how I suffered and made good on his promise to kill his father if he hurt me again.

The moments both men left me in peace, giving me the house to myself, gave me rest if only for a time. Sometimes they would leave for an hour or more, fishing, searching out new trapping lines—or whatever they called it.

Giddy, I would hum and hurry to finish my chores, grab a book, and curl up on Flynn's bed.

Because it smelled like his skin.

Because it didn't remind me of my husband.

Because I could read my smutty stories and fantasize about gentle hands and soft lips. Being on the receiving end of a giving man rather than selfish taking.

I kept the windows wide open so at the first hint of approaching feet, I could leap up and grab up the coffee tin I kept at the ready for such occurrences.

Callan liked his coffee. All day, every day. Having a fresh pot seemed to dampen his pissy attitude the slightest bit. I never did get a word of thanks for being so thoughtful I kept a pot ready, and I eventually stopped expecting it.

The making of the coffee on such days was to hide the fact I'd been lazing around—and becoming aroused over a man who wasn't my husband.

My only joyous times. My only escape.

I clung to them with a stubbornness I didn't realize I had inside me, even tucking a book inside a basket while traipsing up the hill to gather berries once they ripened. From my vantage point, I could keep an eye on Callan through the brambles, hiding out on the back side to re-read another book.

I found the throne-like rock Flynn's Ma had drawn in the image of her son and Dog. Although stone, the seat proved comfortable and afforded me that view of the homestead below while the brush provided enough cover I stayed hidden from sight.

"Saige!"

I jerked my focus off my favorite paperback and peered through the brambles I'd already picked clean, warmth tingling between my thighs over the dirty-talking hero and how he focused on his woman, never giving over to his own need for release until making sure he satisfied her.

Callan stood, hands on hip, glaring up the hill.

Pushing up to my feet, I tamped down the warmth, the happiness I'd felt. "Yes?" I called out, rounding the bush I'd hidden behind, basket in hand.

Callan waved me down.

Letting out a heavy sigh, I did as told, watching him disappear into the cabin. He and Flynn had been fishing, but the younger man wasn't down near the river from what I could see.

He sat at the table, a blood-soaked towel wrapped around his hand.

"What did you do?" I set down the basket, eyeing the blood and trying not to let my stomach empty.

I hated the sight of blood.

"Cleaning fish."

"Daydreaming like his Ma," Callan jumped in, his tone hard as always when putting his son down.

Flynn's lips twitched as though his father's words hit him

like a compliment rather than the negativity Callan had definitely gone for.

"Stitch him up."

Oh God. I swallowed against rising nausea, but rubbed my damp palms on my shorts and headed into the bedroom for my sewing supplies and the first aid kit.

I'd altered clothing from second-hand shops before, but had never sewn...skin.

My stomach heaved, but I didn't have a choice. No way in hell would I tell Callan that I couldn't. No way in hell would I leave Flynn's injury to his father's care.

Teeth clenched and breathing through my nose, I settled at the table beside him. Callan hovered close by.

"Can you heat some water, please?" I asked him, unwrapping the towel around Flynn's hand.

Surprisingly, Callan did as I asked, and I bit back a whimper at the slice across the meaty part beneath Flynn's thumb. He'd cut deep, but at least it was only flesh, no tendons. A clean cut. No jagged edges.

An easy couple of stitches.

Still, my stomach roiled, and I swallowed against the need to vomit.

"Okay." I let out a heavy exhale, refusing to look at the hulking man in front of me or the one clanking around in the kitchen area behind me.

"Have you done this before?" Flynn asked, his voice low but steady.

"No," I whispered, wiping my best needle with an alcohol pad.

My already shot to shit nerves heightened to the whimpering point when I had to touch Flynn's skin for the second time since we'd met. Like a live-wire grazing along my fingertips, the warmth of his wrist shot delicious heat through me. Flynn's lack of reaction sent an ache through my chest I quickly squashed down in thankfulness he did better at controlling his emotions than I.

Or perhaps, he no longer craved me like I felt sure he did those first few weeks I'd come to the homestead.

Lower lip between my teeth, I bit down in attempts to keep the sounds of needy want to rise from inside me as potent energy continued to flicker up my arm and straight down between my thighs.

I cleaned up his wound the best I could with my shaking hands and the water Callan heated. Dousing the area afterward with hydrogen peroxide didn't twitch Flynn's skin beneath my touch.

Rock.

Lower lip between my teeth, I held my breath and slid the needle through Flynn's flesh. He didn't give a verbal or physical response, but I felt enough emotion and reaction for both of us.

Pull through to the knot. Another poke of flesh and pull. Another.

Slow and methodical, head bent to my task, I made tiny x's of black thread in toughened flesh, growing half-giddy with pride over not spewing my lunch all over Flynn's lap.

His lap...a mere foot away.

Arousal returned with a rush as I inhaled until it hurt, Flynn's woodsy scent overpowered the coppery tang in the air. Warmth and hunger rose in a choking, delicious need even more than the brush of our skin, shifting me on my chair.

Our thighs bumped, sending sparks skittering over my body.

My heart beat heavier in my chest with every passing second as I fought to focus. Slowly...thoroughly. One stitch at a time while fighting to breathe in a steady way that wouldn't arouse Callan's suspicion from where his dark shroud of energy hovered over my back.

"Goddamnit, woman," he grumbled. "You're slow as shit."

"I'm just trying to do a good job," I told him without looking away from Flynn's wound. "If I mess this up and infection sets in, Flynn's healing time will be twice as long—if not longer."

An excuse to sit close and breathe him in, one Callan would easily swallow seeing as how he'd want his son healed up and back to work as quickly as possible.

He muttered something under his breath about his lazy son and worthless wife—and surprisingly took his ass outside, leaving us alone.

In close proximity. Too close. The oxygen inside the cabin lessened considerably.

"You need to be careful up there around the brambles," Flynn said before I could spew nonsense to keep the sexual tension rising between us from becoming unbearable silence.

"Why's that?"

"Bears like berries too," Flynn murmured, his low voice tingling over my skin. "They come sniffing around or you hear a grunt, get your backside home. Otherwise, I'll have to track down whichever one hurts you and take him apart piece by piece."

"Are you a good tracker?" I asked rather than focus on the intensity of his sworn statement.

"It's the only thing Pa says I'm good at." He didn't hesitate to answer, but no pride came through in his voice.

But if Callan had said Flynn was good at something, he must be.

I nodded, focusing on my work. "So what do bears sound like—so I know what to listen for?"

A snuffled snort left him, and I bit back a sudden giggle as he grunted a bit, sounding exactly like a wild animal—at least, what I thought one must sound like. I'd never heard a bear before.

"You sound like a real animal."

"Ma always called me a wildling," he said, pain in his voice, but I couldn't bring myself to look in his face. "Born of nature, feral as a fox."

"Tell me about her?" I asked, wanting to know more —know *him*.

Flynn sat silent long enough I glanced up at him. He stared at my hand on his wrist, his brow slightly furrowed, but no emotion in his eyes.

"She taught me to read—not that it does me much good out here." He lifted his focus to my face. "I've read that gardening book you brought along. Would you mind if I tried one of your novels?"

An audible gulp escaped me, and heat flooded my face. I once more bent to my task. "I-I'm not sure you'd enjoy them."

"Why?"

"Well...they're romance?" I squeaked my reply, more like a question than fact.

"So."

"Love stories." I swallowed, pulling the thread taut. "With...*you know*."

"What?"

God. I wanted to sink clear through the floor. "With sex," I managed another squeak.

"Is it good?"

My head jerked up, but no teasing lit his eyes, no hint of

what he truly meant. Or perhaps my brain took me a different route than what he *had* meant. "What?"

"The sex between the characters. Is it good?"

Breath leaving in a rush, I bit back a half-hysterical giggle. "Yes."

"Is it good for you with..."

I followed Flynn's gaze to the window. I adored his innocence, his bluntness, even though it heated my face to what had to be beet red.

"No," I whispered my confession.

"Sometimes, it sounds like you enjoy it." Those mossy green eyes returned to my face, studying with that bland look I hated.

"Y-you hear us."

"Yes, but don't be embarrassed." His focus dropped to my lips. "I like hearing you. The sounds from your mouth... make me hungry."

My pussy pulsed, and I straightened in my chair, hoping to keep from swooning. So much for thoughts over his not wanting me anymore.

"Flynn, that's kind of inappropriate." My voice shook as much as the needle clutched in my hand.

"I'm sorry." He tore his focus off my face for the window again. "I shouldn't have said that."

I bit my lower lip and blinked down at the hand I still needed to finish stitching.

"Why do you bite your lip like that that if what I said is so wrong?" Flynn's soft voice hit my ears a heartbeat before his fingertip gently touched my crooked tooth, holding tight to my lip.

Pulling back a few inches dropped his hand from my mouth, and I found myself studying his face. Losing myself in the heat he allowed to fill his eyes.

"Because, your words make me...*hungry*," I repeated his word in a whisper.

Tense heaviness settled over us, my heightened breaths loud in my ears along with the boom of my heart thundering in my chest.

Flynn shifted, using his free hand to adjust the bulge in his pants.

Oh God.

Hand shaking, I knotted the final stitch, and pushed away from the table, half expecting my knocking knees to drop me to the floor.

"You'll need to keep your hand clean," I rushed to say, my voice shaky as hell as I dropped my needle in the bowl with the reddened, cooled water. "Keep it wrapped for a day or two. No chopping wood. No—"

"Saige."

I stopped with my rushing words, but couldn't bear to turn to face him.

"If Pa had been serious in his offer to share when you first arrived—would you have told me what to do? Would you have shown me how to touch you? Kiss you? Give you pleasure Pa tells me a woman can have?"

I swallowed against the whimper wanting to eek through my tightening throat. Flynn had been nothing but honest with me, earning my trust. How could I possibly lie? "Yes."

He left me without another word, and I grasped hold of the table to keep from toppling over with weakness, and the most arousing need I'd never felt.

A *dangerous* need, an emotion I couldn't put words to, flooded through me. No matter my stoicism in keeping from Flynn, his draw couldn't be ignored.

There was no denying we headed toward trouble.

15

FLYNN

I needed space.

Needed to breathe in air not tinted with Saige's sweet scent, fill my eyes with beauty outside a long braid I thought about fisting while feasting on her neck. Her bright eyes, full of that same hunger raging through me that I tried to hide, brought me to the edge of my sanity.

Since my wounded hand kept me from being useful to Pa, I grabbed up my pack right after we ate and headed to the hills without a word. Not even a thanks for dinner or for stitching me up. Couldn't speak one word her way—couldn't even look at her, or I felt sure I'd ravage her, fuck the fact she didn't belong to me.

Pa saw me go. Saw my pack, rifle slung over my shoulder, and Dog totting at my side.

He didn't stop me from going, didn't spew his usual shit over my heading out—but I wouldn't have stopped even if he had. Usually, he'd come after me if he saw me sneaking off, but the fact I didn't hide it, the fact I'd held his gaze while tossing food into a sack said it all.

I hadn't shied from him since his return from town.

Hadn't given an inch to the expression inside me, wanting to make itself known on my face whenever he tried to get his digs in. I'd turned eighteen, had become a man, one hardened to the point I knew how to hide it. But then, I'd had years of practice.

He hadn't once raised his hand to me since he'd come back—hadn't to his young wife either, thank fuck. I'd promised to see him through life, but if he left bruises on her like he'd done Ma, I felt sure I'd go back on my word.

Ma would have to forgive me from the grave.

But he'd been on good behavior other than his mouth running. Maybe he'd changed like I had in his absence. I had to trust that thought so I could escape before the need to fuck turned me into a raging animal.

Maybe Saige's softness *had* rubbed off on him, and that's what kept him from becoming physical with her. The thought of her rubbing anywhere near me had me hard and aching every time my thoughts lingered on her thighs that disappeared beneath the hem of her shorts.

I sprawled on my back beneath the stars beside the waterfall our first night out, Dog ignoring my good hand fisting my cock, ignoring my grunt as white spurts shot up from my throbbing dick. He didn't so much as twitch a whisker as I groaned out Saige's name.

Shame should have filled me, hot and heavy, but as Pa had said last fall when he returned from town, I couldn't give two fucks. I couldn't control the animalistic need inside me for Saige, so why bother trying?

I also couldn't stand the thought of being too far in case she needed me.

Rather than head deeper into the wilderness, I stayed put at the waterfall. Plenty of fish to eat, and snares caught me some small game to roast over the open fire.

I'd built a sturdy lean-to out of downed wood years earlier, and a few new pine boughs atop and beneath fixed it up for my stay. A few apples and jerky were the only foods I'd snagged before taking off, but I would make do.

Always did.

Swimming in the pool beneath the waterfall cooled my heated skin whenever memory and need took me to the breaking point. Straight off the mountain, the waterfall held a teeth-chattering cold that would shrivel any man's balls up tight. The clean water also helped me keep my wound free from infection, and within a week, I used the tip of my knife to rid my skin of the tiny stitches Saige had labored over.

Such care. Her soft touch.

I couldn't believe Pa hadn't pointed out my hard dick and attempted to wound me with teasing. While I might have learned how to shut out the outward effect of his words on me, they still hurt worse than fists.

Always had.

Oftentimes, I wondered if Ma had felt the same. Had she lived longer, I would have had a confidant, a bond over shared hurt, not just blood. Eventually, one of us would have stood up to Pa for the other, either ending his mistreatment, or in my case, probably ending *him*.

I considered how Pa spoke to Saige, and even though he hadn't shown signs of wanting to hit her, I wondered if he would eventually take his fists to her like he'd done to Ma and me before I'd outgrown him.

"What do you think, Dog?"

The beagle side-eyed me from where he sat while I whittled a stick to pass the time.

"You don't think he'll hurt her, do you?"

Anger and fear swirled in a toxic brew inside my gut, but

I feared my reaction to Saige being within touching distance.

"Can't go back yet," I told Dog through clenched teeth. "Don't trust myself to keep away from her."

Dog circled around me where I sat by our fire and settled against my right thigh, chin on his paws.

"You're a good boy," I told him, patting his flank. "Don't know what I'd do without you."

A sneeze exploded from his nose, and I let out a rare chuckle while he licked his snout clean.

"Love you, dog."

The only being to hear those words since Ma passed.

Her Irish ballad filled my mind, and I took to humming while whittling. Daydreaming about touching Saige again. But same as always, my happiness faded as worry snuck in.

I shouldn't have left.

I couldn't go back.

The internal war kept me up late into the night.

16

SAIGE

Flynn stayed away longer than I expected, creating a safer environment for me. While my body longed for his return, I realized it would be better for everyone if he got his own place. I considered bringing up the idea of Flynn trying for his own homestead, but expected Callan would question my reasons for wanting him gone. Knowing I wasn't a good enough liar to cover the truth, I decided to keep my mouth shut about the whole situation.

Callan wouldn't want his worker he treated as nothing more than a servant to light out on his own for good, anyway.

I enjoyed the quiet working in my garden, sometimes forcing myself to sing in hopes of it bringing joy like it used to. Nameless tunes, some of my favorites from the radio I'll admit to missing...anything to bring life to my slow-beating heart in my chest that seemed to fade every day that passed without Flynn.

Forcing joy didn't work, and I didn't find any in my daily life as Callan's wife.

He still took rather than shared intimacy with me, and my only lifeline to life became my chickens. The fluff balls had taken on feathers, losing their soft down, but I loved them all the same, and they adored me, or the feed I brought them at least.

I sat cross-legged to watch them eat since Callan fished down by the river. Joc took note of me and clucked a few times, side-eyeing me, before coming closer.

She hopped onto my lap.

"Well, okay," I told her, smiling, thrilled she finally found her way into my arms on her own.

She rubbed her little head against my hand like my mom's dog always did to her, looking for attention. A low cluck left her as I scraped my fingernails down over her feathered head, and her eyelids drifted shut as I stroked along the bottom of her beak.

"Aren't you a little love?" I cooed.

Jack crowed at me as if to say, "Get your own hen!", prancing across the pen as though I'd become a threat. He pecked at Joc as though trying to get her away from the big, bad human.

She hopped up in a flutter of wings and took off after him, chasing him around and clucking.

I laughed out loud for the first time since leaving home as she pranced back to me, her head bopping with every little cluck escaping her beak. She made herself comfortable on my lap again, and I gave her the attention she wanted.

"So you've got an asshole husband, too?" I whispered, still giggling. "You've got more balls than me, though, Joc. I only wish I could fly after Callan and speak my mind when he gives me shit."

Sadly, she didn't respond, but my smile lingered as I

made my way back into the house to make dinner for said asshole.

He traipsed into the cabin not long after I did, bringing the heavy shroud I couldn't ignore. My smile dissolved in a matter of seconds—but he caught sight of my face first.

"The fuck has you smiling like that?"

"The chickens," I didn't hesitate to answer. No harm in letting him know the truth for a change.

"Chickens?"

"Yeah. Joc, actually. The black hen. She's really sweet."

He snorted and set the bucket of fish on the table. "You named the fucking chickens."

It sounded like he laughed at me with his non-question, so I didn't respond, but rather, clamped my lips shut and busied myself making a flour dredge for the fish.

"Been spending a lot of time with them."

I nodded.

"Seems you like them more than me."

My heart rate jacked up, skin pebbled in awareness of where he headed with his words, but I forced out a laugh. "They're just chickens, Callan."

"And you like them more than me."

I rolled my eyes at his attempt to manipulate me—but if the bastard treated me a little better, the fact he spoke wouldn't be the truth. "Don't be silly."

A hand grasped my elbow and spun me before I could find my footing, searing pain registering across my cheek before the sound of his palm across my face.

"Don't give me any sass, woman."

Tears welled my eyes, and I clamped my lids shut, desperate to keep from reacting with fists and shrieks. Doing so would only make things worse. My fingernails dug into my palms beside my hips.

"I-I'm sorry," I whispered, my tight throat making words difficult. Tears escaped down my cheeks as his grasp on my elbow sent pain down to my wrist.

"Taking up with the goddamn chickens—guess you're missing my faggot son."

He's not a faggot. I managed to clamp my teeth shut before spitting that truth out.

"What, Saige? You lonely out here?" He let go of my elbow with a small shove, sending me back against the counter along the wall. My hip bone connected with the edge, and I bit back my gasp. "Best get the fuck over it. You're mine now, and there's no way outta here unless you want to walk for a week straight. Knowing you," he let out his dry laugh, "you'd be lost in a matter of minutes."

Rubbing my hip, I turned back toward my task, wiping my cheek on my shoulder.

"Just going to ignore me?"

"What do you want me to say, Callan?" I refused to look at him while gathering my courage, hand shaking as I dumped some salt into the bowl of flour. "If I say I'm lonely, you'll only make fun of me. If I say I'm not, that I'm content living out here on our homestead, you won't believe me."

"*My* homestead. It isn't yours."

"Your homestead," I amended, the ache in my chest causing more tears to fall. He didn't see me as an equal, as that partner and help mate he'd claimed to want. He'd built me up while dating me, I realized, only to manipulate me into becoming his servant and sex slave.

"I want peas and new potatoes with that there fish."

Lucky for me, I'd gathered enough of both of his favorites already for our dinner.

He left me alone, thank God, and while the tears poured,

I created a meal of perfection even though I rather would have failed on purpose just to piss him off.

But I'd felt the crack of his palm. The beginning of what Flynn's mother must have endured, and I refused to do anything intentionally to earn more of his physical anger.

I'd made my bed—and sleeping in it had become hell.

17

FLYNN

A few more days of sleeplessness, and I felt as though I'd calmed, had gotten hold of myself. I started homeward, the short two miles to Pa's homestead easily eaten up by my long strides.

I decided to stop by Ma's grave near the brambles on the way. Maybe catch a nap in the afternoon sun.

Dog trotted ahead of me as usual, but he pulled up abruptly on alert, ears raised.

"What, boy?" I murmured, slowing to a halt behind him. No sense of danger roused inside me, and I strained my eyes for whatever it was he saw through the brush and wayward trees around us. "What, boy?" I asked again, and he started off, ears still alert, his steps slower.

I stayed close on his heels, and within a matter of seconds, I heard it.

A soft, haunting voice...singing.

My feet stumbled to a halt as the tune rose and fell in familiar notes, bringing pain and happiness in equal, clashing waves.

Ma...

Dog eyed me. Waited, his dark eyes staring me down.

"It's not her," I whispered to him, my chest aching and eyes dampening.

He turned and took a few more steps, and I found myself moving after him, my heart thundering inside my ribs.

I didn't believe in ghosts, but I yearned for Ma's spirit, her touch upon my head, her lips on my cheek.

The sweet voice grew louder, and I stumbled to a stop as Saige came into view.

She wore her long auburn hanging free down her back, a basket draped over her forearm as she picked berries. The song I'd clung to in my mind since Ma's passing came from her lips.

I sank to my knees, sitting back on my haunches, an ache searing through my chest as Saige sang the song of a young fellow who'd mistaken his true love for a swan—and shot her dead.

A morbid tale, a sad tune, but it reminded me of Ma all the same.

Saige's voice faded into the still air as I stared at her, Dog at my side. Her heavy sigh upon finishing reached my ears from the short distance, her shoulders lowered and head tipped down.

I should have grunted and snuffled like a bear to scare her off, but I couldn't bring myself to let her go. She'd brought joy into my life. Sunshine to Pa's darkness. She appreciated my teaching her. She built me up when Pa tore me down.

The ache of memory she'd brought on turned into the need to make Saige smile, to hear her soft laughter that lit up my insides. To seeing another peek of that cute crooked tooth.

My mind went to what used to make me happy—a soft

touch, affection like Ma used to give me, the sense of being filled up to overflowing.

Focused on seeing Saige smile, I stood, my heart beating steadily in my chest. Dog trotted ahead of me, brushing against her legs and startling her from the deep of her mind.

"Oh!" She jerked around to face me, her lips parted and eyes wide as I moved closer, all thoughts shut down, only needing to touch her. To taste her. To make her happy.

Her head tilted back as I stopped before her. A gasp escaped her as I cupped her feather-soft cheek in my palm.

"Flynn," she breathed my name.

"I don't like when you're sad," I whispered. Without giving it a second thought or allowing her time to respond, I bent my head and pressed my lips to hers.

The soft cushion of her mouth parted as I brushed my lips over hers, the scent of berries in her exhale filling my nose and lungs. Her quiet whimper against my mouth roared through me, tightening every muscle, instilling life in my groin, and I grasped her close, my free arm banding around her waist.

Soft curves. Sweet scent.

With a sigh, she grasped at my back, clutching me tight, her head tilting. The flick of her tongue along my lower lip shuddered need through me, deeper and more addictive than any sounds she'd made beyond the wall separating our beds.

My cock strained against my pants, and the gentle movements of her belly against my aching length oozed wetness from its slit. I fought off the instinct to push her to the ground and claim. The instinctive urge to mate. Take.

She caressed my tongue with her own, teaching. Guiding, when I would have gone feral with the lust trying to bust through my skin.

Light-headed, every inch of my body tingling, I damn near lost myself to craving what I couldn't have. Tangling my fist in her hair, diving deep into her mouth to taste and touch all I could reach, barely holding onto sanity. Drinking in her whimpers, every shudder that rippled her tiny form in my arms.

"F-Flynn..." She tore her mouth away, both of us breathless.

Staring, pressed tight against one another, chest to knees. Soft curves and hard flesh tensed and screaming for release.

Lost in the wilderness of her brown eyes, her swollen, black pupils a fathomless depth, I searched to find my soul she'd stolen with my first kiss.

Panted breaths mingled between us, weaving together and giving life to the bond between two hopeless souls.

A wildling of the back country. A hurting woman married to the wrong man.

Two aching hearts desperate for love. Affection.

She pulled away from me, my knuckles grazing down over the swell of her chest as she stepped back. My hand dropped to my side, the tremble through her body as she grabbed up the basket she'd dropped twisting my insides up tight.

A tear slid down her pink cheek.

"Saige," I choked out, but she fled away from me, hair in cascading waves behind her. Hurried footsteps leading her back toward unhappiness.

I'd wanted nothing more than to give her joy—but it seemed I'd only made things worse. She'd given me a taste of what I'd been longing for, but at great cost to herself, I feared.

Fallen short—a failure, just like Pa claimed. I would

never be enough for her, even if she had the freedom to choose. I would never have the means of supporting her like Pa did.

The call of the wilds behind me beckoned, promising solitude. Perhaps a bit of peace.

I took it, the taste of sweet berries still on my tongue, regret sour in my stomach.

SAIGE

Flynn's lips intoxicated. I knew I would want to taste him for the rest of my life.

He'd kissed and wrecked me far beyond what his father's slap had done the day before. Thank God his hit hadn't caused bruising or left a mark after the redness faded. Flynn would have killed him for sure. The berry brambles had been my escape from Callan, but I wouldn't be able to head up the hill again without being haunted by the first brush of Flynn's lips. The softness of his whiskers on my skin, the scent of the wilderness clinging to him as sharply as I'd done with my hands on his back.

Thinking of him had always brought arousal, hot and wet, but his touch brought life to the empty heart inside my chest. Hope had sprung up like a geyser, filling me to near bursting.

One pause for breath from his lips, and reality returned like the river's frigid water.

If only it'd numbed me as bathing in the river did.

I kept my head down while making dinner. Read quietly

in the confines of the cabin while Callan did whatever he did outside until close to bedtime. I crawled into our bed before he did, using a feigned migraine as an excuse, and still my mind ran through my stolen moment with Flynn rather than let me sleep by the time Callan put out the lamp.

Eyes clenched shut, I prayed for just one night of reprieve from his attentions.

The selfish bastard didn't give two shits about my head, not that I'd truly expected him to.

Dry as a bone, unable to entice a bit of moisture between my thighs, his rough taking hurt me deeper than before, and I lay face down on the mattress, choking on sobs until the final thrust and burst of his cum inside me.

My heart pressed heavy into the mattress, the shroud of darkness his presence always brought weighing on my body and mind. I couldn't rouse myself to clean up the mess he'd made, but added silent tears to the sheets.

Within seconds, Callan snored, and I dug my fingernails into my palms to keep from scratching at his face. I imagined digging into the flesh of his cheeks, cramming skin cells and blood beneath my fingernails. Leaving rivulets of blood dripping down into his beard.

The thoughts shouldn't have stirred anything inside me other than disgust and horror. As a timid woman, I'd never hurt a soul—but Callan...

He farted long and loud, let out a groan, and rolled to face me, his snored exhales bathing my face in sour breath. The stench of his gas rose, and I buried my face in my pillow to keep from gagging.

Foul man.

Mean man.

The image of scratching his eyes rose again in my mind, and I had a sudden fit of hysteric giggles burst past my lips. I quickly sobered them lest I wake him up, and more tears squeezed past my clenched eyelids.

Sleep slithered in eventually, cutting off thoughts of maiming Callan to the point he couldn't hurt anyone ever again.

———

Lugging water to the cabin the next day for laundering the cum-stained sheets, had me cursing at myself for being lazy the night before. Scrubbing, wringing, and hanging out linens to dry took an entire morning, and by mid afternoon, I wanted to cry over the fact I still had to cook something for dinner.

God forbid I take it easy and offer a meager sandwich rather than the hot meal my bastard husband always expected.

I poked around the canned goods, hoping for some inspiration. Too late to soak dried beans to make soup. We saved the canned stew for emergencies, I'd been told. My exhaustion wouldn't qualify as a good enough excuse for an easy dinner in his mind.

The open windows let in a pleasant breeze, and I closed my eyes a moment to breathe in the fresh air untainted by exhaust or fumes from restaurants. Trying to count my blessings proved a joke.

My heart ached for Flynn, even though what he'd done was wrong on so many levels. Between my thighs still ached from the night before.

Shoulders sagged, I fought the sting in my eyes, the tightness in my chest.

Jack, the rooster, let out a heavy squawk, and I snorted a sudden giggle, expecting Joc put him in his place. He continued on as though she'd thoroughly pissed him off.

Maybe after dinner I would linger out in the enclosed pen, give the chickens a little treat, and enjoy petting my only friend. A small smile lingering, I pulled down the bin of rice, thinking about making a stir-fry with some greens from the garden.

Callan's footsteps outside the door flatlined my lips, my brow furrowing over the fact Jack still squawked.

"Brought dinner," Callan said as the door opened. His teasing tone skittered shivers down my spine.

I glanced over my shoulder.

He held Joc upside down by her feet—blood dripping from her neck and the dangling head he'd almost sliced clear off.

My breath caught on a gasp at her small head holding on by a mere bit of flesh, and he chuckled, watching me back peddle farther into the cabin, my hands clutching at the shirt covering my pounding heart.

"What did you do?" I cried, my stare on the precious bird he hefted higher to inspect.

"Was in the mood for chicken," he said, turning his gaze on me. "Such a *sweet* thing—I'm sure she'll be tender and delicious."

Tears rolled down my cheeks as he stomped into the cabin and tossed Joc's body onto the table with a thump, splattering blood everywhere.

"Pluck her good," he said with another laugh, turning once more for the door. "And make sure you crisp up that skin golden brown—but keep the meat juicy."

Beautiful black feathers...dark blood. Lifeless eyes, half-lidded.

The door slammed shut behind him, and I sobbed, stuffing a fist against my mouth, desperate to keep my emotions bottled as I rocked back and forth.

Fucking bastard!

Keening escaped around my knuckles, and I bit down hard.

How could he do such a thing? How could he be such a vile human being?

It took me a full ten minutes of imagining stabbing the butcher's knife into his throat over, and over again, before I could force my feet to move. Even if I truly wanted to kill my husband over taking my favorite thing other than Flynn on the homestead from me, I knew I could never accomplish the deed.

He outweighed me by a good hundred pounds if not more.

Feeling as though my muscles wanted to jump from beneath my skin, I forced my feet to take me to Joc's side, knowing I didn't have a choice.

My fucking husband wanted chicken for dinner—and a dead bird lay on the table, the opportunity to satisfy him.

I'd rather claw his eyes out.

Tears poured from mine, and I tried to slow my shuddering breaths while trailing my fingertips over Joc's still feathers.

No more shared secrets. No other reason to smile...

I cradled her up in my arms, her still warm blood soaking into my shirt, and sniffed my running nose clear so I could lean down and kiss her soft feathered back without dripping snot onto her.

"I hope you give him the worst indigestion ever, Joc. Turn rancid in his gut and give him pain like the kind stabbing my heart. Turn his bowels to water and drain him of life."

She didn't cluck back, and five minutes later, after saying my goodbyes, I forced myself outdoors to clean her properly to prepare the dinner I had no intention of eating.

19

FLYNN

Worry over how Saige had run from me kept me awake long into the night as Dog slumbered against my side.

Had she returned to the cabin with tears still rolling down her cheeks? If so, Pa would have taken note. He would have poked and prodded. Maybe teased or gave her a hard time.

I shouldn't have left again. I should have followed on her heels, apologized, and made sure things were okay between us—and with her—before allowing her anywhere near that prick. And until I had that thought, it was too late. Both she and Pa would have been in bed for a few hours.

In the morning, I hoofed it homeward, but slowed my steps upon seeing Saige doing laundry in the barrel out front of the cabin.

Pa worked on digging a new hole for the outhouse that needed to be moved, and if I continued on my course, I'd end up finishing for him.

I settled onto Ma's rock, elbows on knees while leaning down to watch Saige work. While not the fastest worker, she didn't waste any moves, her energy focused and making sure she thoroughly accomplished her task—another part of her Pa didn't appreciate.

I'd heard him grumble about her slow ass more than once, but what rush could there be living out in the wilds unless scrambling to get firewood stored up? What awaited her after laundering?

The garden sprouted green and lush, rumbling my stomach for fresh food. Saige's chickens pecked around at the ground, their pen too far away for the clucks to reach me.

Dog let out a sigh and settled onto the ground, flitting the memory of Ma's drawing through my mind. She'd drawn me sitting here.

I settled my hand atop the arm rests she'd stacked, the stone cool beneath my calloused palm. The left wobbled a bit, but held steady.

My attention roamed to her headstone a little ways away, and sudden exhaustion sagged my shoulders stretching out the flannel covering them. Eyes closing, I tried to recall her fingers in my hair. Her smile. The light in her green eyes that mine didn't hold, no matter how similar we looked. I didn't have a true image of her hidden away—Pa had burned all of her stuff after her death while muttering about her leaving him, too—but I remembered the soft curve of her lips when she'd smile at me, and the plumping of her cheeks when she laughed at my wildness.

Traipsing barefoot across dirt and stone. Ripping holes in my pants and the elbows of my shirts from tumbling and crawling around like an animal with Dog.

Miss you so damn much, Ma.

Letting out a heavy exhale, I returned my focus on Saige. She wrung out what looked like the sheet from their bed.

Pa still used the spade on the earth.

Seeing Saige would be safe for a time, I shuffled over to Ma's grave and sat in the weeds, plucking the ones against her headstone. No name, no date. Just a slab of stone I'd lugged to the spot five years or so after her death, when I'd been strong enough to do so.

"You would like Saige, Ma," I told the stone, imagining she listened. "She's a kind woman, same as you. Sweet and timid. Easy pickings for Pa, unfortunately. Kinda wish she'd never come out here. I don't like the way Pa talks to her— same as he did to you."

I plucked another weed and flicked it away.

"If he ever lays a hand on her, though, I won't be too afraid to defend her like I was with you. I should have stood up to him. Should have done more to stop his hurting you. Should have snuck a radio call into town to get you some help when you got sick. I was a chicken shit, Ma. I won't be that for Saige if things get physical between them."

Laying on my back, I gazed up into the sky, deciding I would wait for Pa to finish what he'd set out to accomplish for the day. As long as I didn't hear any hollering or crying, I'd stay put—and hoof it down to the homestead in time for dinner.

My stomach growled, but I decided to rest a bit before heading home.

———

I opened my eyes, the dimness in the sky telling me I'd slept longer than expected. Pushing up to my feet, I stretched and yawned, feeling better than I had in days.

My hand didn't hurt, even though a nice scar bumped the skin where Saige had sewn me up.

Dog let out a yawn, too, his dark eyes peering up at me as I slung my backpack off Ma's rock onto my back and grabbed my rifle.

"Let's get on home, Dog. Get us some dinner."

He trotted off down the path like he knew what I'd said, and I took in the sheets hanging out in the breeze. Pa worked out by the woodshed, sawing some lumber, so Saige hadn't yet called him in for dinner.

Stomach once more growling, I looked forward to real food almost as much as seeing Saige's face again. I expected she wouldn't look at me, but it would be for the best. I hadn't read too many books in my life, but Saige's eyes came as easily as placing the ABCs in order. An open book, Ma would say, same as she'd said of me in my younger years.

Thank God I'd learned to shut down, hide away my feelings from my face, or life would be even more of a hell living with Pa. I'd adopted his bored expression—learned it from the very best.

He couldn't hide his anger though, and I caught sight of it the second he heard me approaching and lifted his head from where he measured another rough-hewn piece of lumber.

"About time," he said, eyeing the state of my filthy pants. "Been working my ass off the past week, doing what you should have been. Next time you run off like that, don't bother coming back. I'm not some tit for you to suck off, faggot boy. Understand?"

I nodded, taking care to not grit my teeth, allowing him to see the telltale twitch of my beard like his always did when he got angry.

"Hope you're hungry," he said, his lip curling to twitch his beard in a different way all together. "Gonna be one hell of a dinner tonight."

I didn't ask, but moved on past him, heading down to the river to wash up.

Pa already went inside by the time I finished, and the second I opened the door, a blast of warm, delicious air hit me in the face.

Chicken. Something we only ever had after Pa went into town.

My mouth set to drooling, and I set my bag on the floor while closing the door.

Saige stood with her back to me, not turning to acknowledge my arrival. Just as well.

"Smells good in here," I said, pulling out my chair.

She'd already set a third place, so Pa must have told her I'd come home.

I'd expected pink cheeks, but a sickly, pale color had taken over her face when she turned. Head down, as always, she considered the fried chicken she held on the platter in her shaking hands.

She set it in front of Pa and slid into her chair, half-curled in on herself, shoulders hunched, hands in her lap.

I knew better than to ask what bothered her, but I did a quick inspection of her down-turned face for bruises—not a one.

Pa chuckled as he speared a chicken breast with his fork. "Looks good, doesn't it?"

"Yes, sir." I eyed the platter he held, my fingers itching to get my hands on it.

Took him long enough, but he finally handed it over.

"It's Joc." Saige's whisper paused my fork from stabbing a thigh.

She'd lifted her head, her watery eyes staring at the plate in my hand.

Joc. Her favorite hen.

Oh, fuck.

My mouth dried right fuckin' out as I realized what Pa had done.

Pa laughed as I eyed him, fighting to keep sane, and he lifted the breast in his hands. "Welcome home, son."

20

SAIGE

I shouldn't have told Flynn. I should have kept my lips clamped shut, but my heart continued to break, and I couldn't bear the thought of keeping it in. Desperate for compassion, for someone to know my devastation, I told him who he was about to eat.

Flynn stilled, but his face remained passive when I dared a glance his way. His scraggly beard twitched, but no other evidence of emotion moved him. He speared a thigh and put it on his plate before handing the platter over to me.

Callan chuckled again, but Flynn held my gaze as he seemed to do so easily, a quick flash of pity atop anger resting in his green orbs.

He didn't speak a word, but I swore I heard his thoughts clear through my head—I'd lost weight—I needed to eat. Take the gift of Joc's life into my mouth and let Callan know he couldn't keep me down.

My hands shook, but I took the chicken, setting it with in a clatter in the middle of the table.

Callan snickered when I lifted one of Joc's leg between two fingers and moved it onto my plate, my stomach roiling.

Rice and more snap peas found their way alongside the meat as my mindlessness and numb hands went to work doing what I felt sure Flynn wanted me to do.

He cared about my wellbeing.

A tear slid down my cheek as I cut a hunk of Joc off the bone, and my stomach rolled the second I put the bite in my mouth. Breathing heavy through my nose, I chewed slowly, trying to ignore the burst of flavor I hadn't enjoyed since I'd first moved to the homestead.

I'm sorry, Joc.

"Good, isn't she?" Callan asked. "So *sweet*."

Neither Flynn nor I responded, even though I watched him from the corner of my eye. He ate like a starved man. I choked the first bite down and guzzled some water to wash away the taste—even if it made my mouth salivate for more.

Guilt over enjoying that bite tightened my stomach to the point of pain, so I bypassed the leg and focused on the rice and peas. I managed all of three or four bites in the time it took Callan to finish dinner, his stare heating my face.

"Don't let it go to waste," Flynn said quietly, drawing my head up. Warmth filled his eyes, although a hint of the pity remained. "We rarely get chicken out here, so try to take some happiness in Joc's sacrifice."

"We got two others ready for eating out in the pen," Callan argued.

"And we'll need one to lay eggs and the other to fertilize them," Flynn stated without a hint of a bite in his tone, even though energy seemed to crackle off him.

Callan's darkness hung over the table, and I held my breath. Waiting for Flynn to earn what he had coming to him from back talking to his Pa.

Sass had earned me a slap—but it appeared Callan

knew better than to attempt taking on his younger, bigger son. He kept his hands to himself. His mouth shut.

A few seconds of tense silence, and Callan pushed back from the table to retrieve his pipe he enjoyed smoking on the stoop.

"Are you going to be alright?" Flynn whispered once his father left us.

I nodded.

"I'm sorry he's such an ass."

"It's not your fault."

"Still." Flynn set his silverware atop his empty plate and took it over to the bucket I used to wash dishes. He grabbed up his pack from where he'd dropped it by the door and put things away while I cleaned up.

"Would it upset you if I said dinner really was the best thing I've ever tasted?" he asked quietly while pouring himself more water.

I slowly dried my hands on the dish towel, considering his question, my emotions, and my reactions to eating one of my pets. "No," I finally whispered my answer. "You were right—we should take every small happiness we can."

Forcing my head up, I met his steady gaze. Mossy-green eyes, unshuttered. Open for me to read, and the desire he held for me clenched my thighs.

"That song you were singing..." Flynn swallowed and glanced out the window beside us. "My Ma used to sing it all the time. Hearing it again broke my heart and mended it all at the same time."

My throat tightened, and as he once more looked down at me, warmth rose to flush my skin and quicken my heart.

He rubbed his lips together while glancing down at mine.

I held my breath, but couldn't back away. Didn't want to.

"Thank you," he whispered and stepped back, allowing me to suck in a breath which stalled at the slight smile on his lips. Small lines at the corners of his eyes—he'd never been anything but serious, so bland, not showing emotion.

But he let me in for a brief moment, offering kindness yet again, even after I'd run away from him.

Spinning on his heel, he made for the front door and left me alone, still emotionally charged from exhaustion, desire for him, and hatred for my husband.

Take happiness... Shaking my head, I hung up the towel to dry.

———

Flynn took his pillow and blankets to the woodshed. He'd come back home from wherever he'd gone, but I guess he wasn't too thrilled about hearing his father fucking me after the kiss we'd shared up behind the berry brambles.

I wasn't too keen on my husband touching me either, and the second he crawled into our bed and grabbed my ass, I scooted away, my heart pounding. "Not tonight."

"Bleeding?"

"Yes," I lied, keeping my voice steady.

With a curse, he rolled away from me, and I held in my sigh of relief.

Tension still kept me from rest, however, and Callan's snoring a few hours later, added to my busy mind.

Night had settled over the cabin, and I lay without moving, thinking of Flynn on his pallet out in the shed. Dog would probably be curled up beside him. Envious of the animal, I wondered what it would feel like to cuddle. Hug and pet with affection on someone who wanted it, someone who would appreciate and reciprocate.

Physical love—I couldn't imagine the joy it would bring if one mere kiss had turned my world on its axis.

Longing beyond the need for physical love swelled inside me to the point I couldn't keep still.

Tears stung my eyes, and I let out a slow, steady breath. I rolled from bed. Tiptoed across the cabin. Let myself out into the stillness of the wilderness in nothing more than my night shirt.

Heart thumping in my chest, I crept barefoot across the moonlit ground, knowing what I wanted was wrong, but too heart-broken and tired to avoid the temptation of what called to me. Of what I knew could be found if I attempted to take what happiness I could find.

The woodshed door sat open by a few inches, as though Flynn had expected me.

I pushed it inward, and Dog lifted his head but didn't make a sound.

Flynn rolled onto his back. I could barely make out his face in the darkness. He didn't speak—simply held out his hand.

Beyond caring about ethics or morals, I didn't hesitate to step close, clasp my hand in his, and sink to my knees onto the blankets beside him.

He sat, and we peered at one another in the darkness, his free hand brushing my long hair over my shoulder.

"We shouldn't," he said, his low, shaky tone pebbling my nipples.

"I'm going to take my happiness when I can," I whispered back, my heart in my throat.

"Then let's have tonight—right now—since we can't have tomorrow."

I nodded, but I wanted tomorrow. And the next day.

Flynn cradled my face in his hands and leaned in to claim my lips.

Claiming—no other word for the swift pressure, the hunger of his tongue seeking mine. A whimper escaped me, and I placed my hands on his bare chest.

Hot. Hard muscle flexing beneath my touch.

I committed every swipe of his lips to memory, every nip of his teeth deep inside my head for the times I needed help to endure the life I'd chosen.

Wetness soaked me between the thighs as he groaned into my mouth, both of us hardly experienced, but hungry all the same, the desperation between us heavy enough to taste in the charged air between us.

He fisted my hair, yanking my head back to kiss along my jaw, and I pulled on his beard, bringing his mouth back to mine.

"Show me how to touch you, Saige," he said against my lips. "Show me how to please you."

A sudden sob rose to my lips, but I held it in, grasping his hand, and placing it on my breast.

Both of us gasped in a breath, our kiss halting. Noses brushing. Shared exhales at the same time.

"So soft," he murmured, and I clutched his shoulder as he held me through my shirt, his thumb gently rubbing over my aching peak.

Not enough—not close enough.

I leaned back, ripped my shirt off overhead, and pulled his hand back to my breast, heavy pants still escaping my mouth. He grasped the other on his own, and I peered at him through the darkness, barely making out his eyes that focused on what he held in his hands.

"You like this."

"Yes," I whispered, even though he hadn't asked a question. I shifted closer, once more reaching to touch his chest. My fingertips explored over his pectorals—hairless and sculpted from laboring only the way a mountain man could. Ripples of muscles down his core—flinching and jumping with every brush of my fingers.

He rolled my nipples, causing another rush of wetness to soak my panties. "I want to taste you," he groaned out, and I lowered myself to lie down alongside him.

Leaning over me shifted the blanket from his hips, and hard, hot flesh slid along my thigh at the same time he covered my aching nipple with his mouth.

Brushing whiskers, wet flicks of his tongue, gentle suction...

"Flynn." I grasped his hair and moved my hips, seeking relief from the zinging need shooting from my breast to my clit, so needy for him to fill me, I couldn't keep from whimpering.

As though reading my mind, he slid a hand down over my spasming belly and cupped the apex of my thighs, a deep groan rumbling his chest. The suction on my nipple intensified, the scrape of his teeth arching my back as I held him tightly to me.

He rubbed his palm down over me, strong, roughened fingertips sliding up and down over my soaked panties.

"Need," I gasped as he once more cupped me fully and dug his hard length into my thigh. "T-take them off. Please."

Flynn sat back abruptly, his hands shaking as he gently slid my panties down my thighs. "You drive me crazy, Saige. Out of my goddamn mind—like a fuckin' animal." Grasping my freed panties, he lifted them to his nose, inhaling and exhaling a groan. "Fuck." His muttered whisper rolled arousal over me, my hips moving as though he already filled me.

"Flynn," I whimpered, fingers digging into his blanket beneath me.

Dropping my panties aside, he grasped one of my thighs and pushed it wide, his calloused hand sending goose-bumps skittering down my leg.

"What I wouldn't do to see you like this beneath the sun." He ran his hand back up my leg, thumbing along the crease at the top. "So beautiful. So perfect." Shifting his thumb took him up through my gaping, soaked lips, to the hard nub at the top.

"Oh!" I shuddered, back arching.

"This?" He repeated the action, and I bit my lip, nodding. "It feels good?"

"Yes," I gasped out as he grazed over my clit with his thumb nail.

Another slow glide down and back up through my wetness, and I'd had about enough of the damn teasing. "Need you, Flynn. Please."

He leaned down into my reaching arm, sliding between my welcoming thighs, resting the back of his hard length against my core. "Never done this before," he said, pushing my hair back from my face and cradling my cheeks, his fingers damped with my arousal smearing on my skin. Musky and wet, but I couldn't find it in myself to care. "Don't want to lose control. Hurt you."

"You won't hurt me, Flynn." I touched his whiskered cheek, pulling his face down. "You make my body ache with want," I whispered against his mouth. "It won't hurt me. Promise."

I licked along his lips and reached between us, grasping his cock.

Hung like a horse finally held meaning for me—the bulge in Flynn's pants hadn't lied. But enough wetness dripped from me to ease his way, and I held no bit of fear in my mind or heart of being impaled by him. I craved it with hunger beyond anything I'd imagined.

Shifting my hips notched him against me.

I took his mouth—and he took me in one steady push, stretching me, filling me to the point I lost my breath.

A shudder shook him in my arms, and he groaned into my mouth as I clamped my heels against his ass, pulling him tighter against me.

"Saige," he whispered my name into my mouth like a prayer, and pulled out, the sloppy drag along my walls and lower lips so perfect, so right, tears slid down my cheeks. "I'm hurting you," he strangled out, shaking to a plank over me, his cock barely notched inside me.

"You're making me happy."

Sinking back in, he dipped his head, licking my tears, causing my eyelids to flutter shut.

Filled to the absolute brim with Flynn...wrong. So, so wrong, but I didn't care. The connection between us swelled and faded with every rock of his hips, every brush of his lips, caress of our tongues.

He fit me perfectly. Rushed true joy through my heart and mind.

If loving Flynn was wrong, I would gladly be the first at hell's door once my time on earth expired.

21

FLYNN

The second her wet flesh closed around my cock, holding me in tight heat, my eyes damn near rolled back into my head. Even releasing my pent-up need a few hours earlier before going to bed, I rode the edge of exploding as her body welcomed me fully, my groin resting against her.

I damn near lost it, wrapped up in her arms, the softness of her breasts against my chest, her heels pressed tight against my flexed ass...

She wanted me closer.

"Saige," I managed, lifting on my hands, teeth clenched to keep from going at her like a goddamn animal. Shifting back pulled my aching length almost entirely from her body. A tear glistened on her cheek. "I'm hurting you."

"You're making me happy."

An ache spread through my chest, and I settled back atop her, licking her tears, sinking back into the most divine sense of home I'd ever felt. Steady flexing and retreating rocked Saige against my blankets, and she clutched at me as though afraid of drowning in what rose between us.

Un-nameable emotion, such need, but far beyond just for release, swelled inside me like the river's spring waters. I wanted to burrow deep inside her—her soul, her mind, her heart. Deeper than any tick, than any ground squirrel hidden away in the caverns of its home.

"More, Flynn—please. H-harder."

Groaning, I took her mouth and gave what she asked for, knowing I wouldn't last with deep-seated thrusts, the snap of my hips pressing the head of my cock as far reaching as it could go.

"More..."

Propped on my elbows, I watched her face in the dark, fucking into her harder. Deep enough I bottomed out, deep enough my sanity lingered on the edge of reason.

Lower lip between her teeth, she peered up at me. Her timid nature had fled in my arms, and she held my stare, holding me captive in her brown orbs nearly overrun with the black of her pupils.

I rocked against her, picking up the pace of my retreat and plunging back in as her heels demanded. My balls drew up tight against my body. Hardened and ready to let loose.

Teeth clenched, mind focused on pleasing her, I thrust faster, her gasps, her fingernails digging into my shoulders, drawing a darkness deep inside me to the surface.

Claim. Own. I wanted to pound her essence into my blankets where she wouldn't find escape.

"Tell me what to do," I gasped out, heaving for breath, giving her all I had—all I could think she needed. "Show me, Saige. Fuck, tell me what to do!"

She wiggled her hand between us, and I tightened my stomach muscles to give her arm room.

The hard nub—her clit. Of course.

"Yes," I grunted, slamming into her, taking note of how

her fingertips fluttered against her clit. "Yes, Saige. Make yourself come."

She gasped, loosening her teeth's hold on her lower lip, and her back arched. "Flynn!" She gasped out my name, and her pussy poured wetness around me, spasming and clutching at my thrusting length.

Yes.

I took her mouth, possessive. Demanding. Tasting her cries, swallowing the exhales she let out between my lips. My hips moved on their own, born of the wilds, the animal nature taking over that of human.

Every thrust moved her along my blankets, and I planted my elbows above her shoulders as she continued to clutch at me, holding her in place for me to fuck into over, and over again.

Mine.

Perfection.

So soft, so sweet.

A grunt, and I buried deep, the first shot of cum through my shaft like a damn geyser, coating every inch of her pussy, a mess following along as I dragged out and shoved back in on another spurt. A third. A damn fourth that sagged me against her, forehead pressed to hers, our haggard breaths mingling in the short distance between our mouths.

My ears rang. Shudders rippled down over me, flexing my ass in attempts to push my softening dick in deeper to trap my cum inside her.

I groaned and rested, burying my face in her neck. "Did I hurt you?"

"No." She caressed down my back with her gentle hands, her ankles still firmly wrapped around my backside.

Our breaths slowed as I breathed her in, memorized the feel of her wetness around my softened cock. How perfectly she cradled my body between her thighs. How perfectly her trailing fingers along my spine brought sighs to my lips.

I could drown in her affection. Submerge myself to the point of pain, of sorrow. In that moment, I knew I would never get enough of her. Never have my fill of feeling her beneath me, hearing my name on her lips, being the one to bring her happiness.

"Please don't leave me again."

Her soft whisper sifted through the haze of contentment in my mind, and the reality of what we'd done settled like a heavy blanket of snow. Coldness crept into my mind, and I tensed.

"Flynn."

"I'm sorry."

"Please don't say that," she said, grasping my beard to pull my face from her neck, her eyes searching my face in the darkness. "Please, Flynn."

"We shouldn't have done this—I should have sent you back. If he finds out..."

I attempted to lift off her, but she clung to me with a fierce strength I hadn't known she'd possessed. "You said we should take our happiness when we can, well I did. I made the choice to come to you. If anyone should say they're sorry, it's me."

"He can't ever know."

"He won't," she hastened to say. She bit her lip, her eyes welling with tears. "Don't shut me out, Flynn. Please. I can see it even here in the dark. Don't hide your thoughts and emotions from me."

"This can't happen again," I said, my tone firm but quiet, loving yet hating how easily she saw the shift inside me to shut down. I eased my cock from her body, but I couldn't bring myself to move away.

I would take this one happiness and keep it close in my heart, my mind, so I could think on it when I needed her.

Saige finally released her tight hold, and I settled back on my haunches between her spread thighs. The sight of my cum dribbling from her slit captured my attention, flaring my nostrils.

Mine.

Gathering up what had dripped onto my blankets, I didn't even consider my actions—simply shoved it back inside her body with two fingers, putting it back where it belonged.

"Flynn," she groaned a whimper, lifting her hips.

My dick attempted to swell as I reached deep inside her silky body, and I clenched my teeth against the want to take her again.

An obscene wet sound filled my ears as I fucked her pussy with my fingers. "So soft and wet," I groaned, grabbing my stiffening dick with my other hand. "I like seeing my cum leak from you."

"Again, Flynn."

"No," I stated through clenched teeth. "But you can take your happiness one last time—if you're able to."

She didn't hesitate to reach between her thighs, and I studied how she touched the swollen nub at the top of her folds, sprawling out onto my stomach to get a closer look— and rub my dick off against my blankets.

The scent of us filled my lungs, and I breathed us in, leaning closer to rub my nose along the back of her hand, working her clit.

Fuck, she smelled like musky sweetness, so damn good my mouth watered.

My tongue flicked out alongside her fingers, and she gasped, lifting her hips. A nudge of my nose against the hard nub she released, and I lapped upward, seeking out her face in the darkness.

She peered down at me, lips parted, and I ingrained the sight in my mind for later...when she couldn't be beneath me, when I couldn't kiss her soft pussy or lap at the wetness we'd made.

I licked at her clit, and she laid back, eyes closing, back arching. "Flynn..." She groaned, and wetness seeped around my thrusting fingers, that divine clamp of her muscles around me shooting release from my dick as I ground my hips into my blankets.

Still groaning, I clasped her thighs and licked her clean, shoving my nose against her, shoving my tongue into her body, wanting one final taste of her release—her happiness.

22

SAIGE

F lynn tugged my panties back up my thighs without a word. Lifted me from his bed and settled my sleep shirt back over me as I peered up at him, wondering at his mind, hating how no expression showed on his face.

"You need to go back to his bed."

Pain, hot and bright, arched through me at his emotionless words. "Flynn?"

He stepped back. "Go, Saige. And don't come out here again."

He shut me out. He'd said as much, but I thought sure he hadn't meant it, only spewed the words to keep either of us from getting in trouble. The stern set of his face told me all I needed to know.

Flynn didn't want me beyond one quick fuck.

My chest pressed in tightly, as though it wanted to fold in on itself and crush the life inside.

One of the best moments of my entire life, ruined.

Stumbling across the yard toward the cabin, I expected sobs and wails to rise, but nothing choked me. I didn't even fear waking Callan and having him learn the truth—that I'd had another man's dick inside my body—his son's.

No guilt. No remorse. But strangely, no heartache, either. *Shock...*

Recognizing the truth of my mental and emotional health, I pushed into the cabin, hardly caring about keeping quiet, my feet taking me through the bedroom doorway, Callan's snores steady as when I'd left him.

I crawled into bed, facing the wall, dry eyed and empty, all-too aware of the pleasant ache between my thighs.

Sleep didn't come all night, and when Callan rolled to hump my leg in the morning, I lay like a dead fish, reminding him of the lie I'd told the night before—I bled.

He cursed and left me alone.

Brain fuzzy and between my thighs still reminding me of what I'd done, I left our bed the second the cabin door shut behind him.

Coffee—thankfully alone and quiet.

Breakfast—silent at the table with the man who made my heart ache but didn't want me, his father quiet for a change.

Let the chickens out and feed them—minus my Joc to spill all my thoughts out to.

Still no tears.

Mended socks and a shirt.

Pulled weeds in the garden and picked some greens for dinner.

All the while, hand saws and an axe sounded in the background as the two men worked together on building a new outhouse.

My new life, my new normal. Pleasantly numb, but for how long could I keep a lid on the emotions brewing deep inside my subconscious?

Two weeks.

Fourteen days, of which ten Callan had been at me while I'd grown desperate for his son. And since I had zero desire to even think about the only man who could turn me on, Callan's thrusts from behind hurt like hell. My period came for real, and since the inconvenience proved more than he could bear in one month, he made good use of my mouth.

An easier way to get him off, even more pleasant regardless of his musky scent that gagged along with his length shoving against my tonsils. Better than dripping his cum from between my thighs and being too sore to walk.

But the bleeding stopped, and he went back to his ways.

Flynn stayed out in the woodshed, only joining us for meals.

I lost weight to the point my jeans sagged low on my hips and I had to use a length of rope to keep them tied up.

Depression became my best friend.

Callan bitched about the circles under my eyes. He complained my pussy had dried out. He grumbled about how I let myself go, having no desire to bathe, but even my dirtiness didn't keep him from having at me.

"Jessie is flying in here in a couple weeks with our winter supplies."

I lifted my head up from staring at my dinner plate and the fork I'd used to push my food around.

Callan sat back, belched, and wiped the back of his hand across his mouth. "I got a list ready to radio in to her tomorrow. Go over it tonight and add anything I might have missed."

I nodded, returning to the meal I'd been attempting to force down.

"Think we could get some candy, Pa?" Flynn asked quietly from across the table. "Maybe some of those chocolate bars Brock likes?"

"Bad enough I have to buy you a couple new shirts," Callan said, eyeing the worn-through elbows of Flynn's flannel.

"Yes, sir."

A flame flickered to life in my gut, the first emotion I'd felt in days. Lifting my head, I caught my husband's gaze. "I'd like another hen to replace the one you stole from me."

He snorted. "That's what's been up your ass the past couple of weeks, making you frigid again? The goddamn chicken?" His brow furrowed, and he leaned forward, his cold eyes sending a shiver down my spine. "I didn't steal nothing. That damn bird belonged to me, just like everything else on this homestead."

The flame swelled inside me, heating me through from the inside out. I wanted to rage—scream and rip my fingernails down his cheeks. Dig out his eyeballs with my fingertips and shove them down his throat. The urge to take a butcher knife to his calloused fingers and chop them as he'd done Joc's head raged through me.

A warm touch to my knee jolted me from my blood-lust thoughts, bringing my human back to center rather than the vengeful animal inside me wanting revenge against the bastard who'd manipulated me into coming out to the hell hole he called his own.

I didn't dare look at Flynn. Didn't dare acknowledge his attempt to calm me, how his soothing touch warmed me through.

Pushing up from the table, I grabbed my plate and set it on the floor for Dog.

"What are you doing?" Callan asked, his pissy tone hardly fear-inducing as I'm sure he'd intended.

"Not hungry."

"That's a waste of good food!"

"It's not going to waste—see?" I waved at Dog, who chowed down the rabbit stew I'd made.

Callan bitched for a few more seconds about my sassy attitude, but I tuned him out, uncaring of what he thought or said.

Jessie would be flying in supplies.

A lifeline, a chance to escape.

For the first time in weeks, a sense of loss, of heartache beyond depression attempted to swell inside me.

Leaving meant never seeing Flynn again.

Callan gathered his pile and tobacco, and I chanced a look at Flynn for the first time in days. He still sat at the table, but his gaze was on me rather than his plate. For a brief second, I swore I saw pain in his eyes. Longing. But he shut it down, shut me out before I could be sure.

I went back to the dishes and shoved my emotions down once more.

A couple weeks I could handle.

The next morning, Callan made my life a hell of a lot easier—he announced he and Flynn would be heading out to scout out new trap lines for the winter months.

23

FLYNN

I made a fuckin' mess of things, and no matter how my mind tried to come up with some way to make things right, to at least make things better, I couldn't. Being with Saige had been wrong. The best night of my life, the most fulfilling action I'd ever taken, but it couldn't happen again. If Pa ever found out...

Saige moved around as though without thought, without emotion, doing only what needed doing. She'd never been one to smile too often, but her face seemed frozen, her eyes haunted, her lips flatlined. She hardly spoke. Didn't eat.

Pa's killing Joc had damn near ruined Saige, but I'd put the last bullet between her eyes by giving us both the attention and affection we craved, only to yank it away and call it a mistake.

But lust to feel her around me again tempted me to take, regardless of consequences.

I'm no bastard like Pa.

The only thought that kept me from selfishness.

But still, the truth I'd stayed away too long, hadn't been

at the homestead to keep Pa from killing Joc and hurting Saige, damn near split my heart in two.

Saige wasted away, and I wanted nothing more than to get her beneath me again, feel her legs wrap around me, taste her tongue against mine, drown in her scent, lose myself to the wet heat of her pussy.

I wanted inside her head.

I wanted her happy again.

Longed to take all the shit she had going on in her mind and carry it. More than anything, I wanted to take away her pain of losing Joc, the anger I caught sight of while at dinner when her eyes had blazed with the need to stab Pa until he bled out on the floor.

The wildness of the back country had gotten its claws into Saige, a little bit every day it seemed, creating a feral side to her sweet one.

I worried my lip to death considering what to do.

Encourage her to leave with Jessie? Give her the love and attention she desperately needed regardless of consequences? Steal her away for my own, and attempt to make a life together with her from nothing?

The first, I couldn't bear the thought of. The second made my cock hard as a rock. The third wasn't an option, seeing as how I *had* nothing. No means to make money outside trapping, but I had no traps of my own, no means to support her.

I lay on my pallet in the woodshed, the open shutters allowing in light.

"What should I do, Dog?" I asked, scratching the top of his head where he sprawled out beside me, wishing he could answer, could offer advice.

Ma would encourage me to go out and enjoy life—but I didn't want to do that without Saige.

I had no fuckin' clue what to do.

The next morning, Pa and I would take off up the smaller river branch north of the cabin to check out new trapping spots. We'd be gone probably two days, three at the most. Saige would have a rest from Pa.

Normally, I hated going out in the bush with Pa, but getting him away from Saige made the thought of the upcoming trip bearable.

"Stay away from the brambles," I murmured to her while grabbing up my pack from atop my bed in the cabin the next morning. "Bears."

She didn't respond, but the slight dip of her head eased my worry.

"Don't go wandering around, either. Carry that pistol dad hangs by the door and keep this at your waist." I handed over my good knife in its sheath, trusting its sharp blade and jagged backside to rip easily into whatever she wanted it to. "Know how to handle a knife?"

"I can butcher a chicken," she spit out quietly, her gaze wandering after Pa through their bedroom door.

A muscle in my jaw ticked. "I'm so fuckin' sorry he did that to you."

"Not your fault." She took the knife and turned away from me.

Longing to wrap her in my arms damn near took me past the point of caring. One slice of my knife could end Pa. End Saige's suffering. End mine.

But I'd made a promise, and I honored the memory of Ma more than I did my own wants and desires.

"Got that sack of food, woman?" Pa asked as he came into the main area of the cabin.

Saige handed it over without a word.

Pa grabbed her ass, and Saige let out a strangled cry.

Teeth clenched, I tensed to go to her defense, but Pa released her with a dry laugh. "Gonna miss that ass."

I turned away and strode out the door, reminding myself getting Pa out of the cabin meant rest for Saige. At least I could do that much. "Let's go, Pa!" I hollered. *You fuckin' bastard.* "Light's wasting away!"

24

SAIGE

The men left me alone, and the first thing I decided on was to curl up on Flynn's bed and read a fictional character's happily ever-after I'd already read dozens of times before. I disappeared between its bodice-ripping, bare-chested hunk pages, escaping reality until lunch.

Canned peaches made up my meal, and I finally set out to do the day's chores. Tears still pricked my eyes over Joc not clucking to greet me when I opened the chicken coop. Jake eyed me like I'd been the villain, taking his woman from him. He'd only stopped crowing a few hours after Callan took her. I was surprised my bastard husband hadn't killed the rooster for all the ruckus he'd raised in that time.

"Count your feathers lucky," I told him, my tone as dead as the heart in my chest.

I meandered through the garden, plucking a few weeds, lifting my face to the sun as I locked the gate behind me.

Warmth coated my cheeks, my forehead, but couldn't touch the cold inside me. I'd wanted a change from my parents and town and sure as hell had gotten it. Another longing for change welled up inside, clogging my throat.

If there's any god out there...

My heart couldn't even finish the prayer, and my eyelids slid open, the hill and brambles in the distance beckoning.

Flynn had told me to stay away, but I grabbed the pistol and knife from inside the cabin, and set off up the hill, my feet itching to get up there for whatever it was leading me. Seeing as how the berry season drew to a close, I didn't expect to fill a basket, so I went without.

What still lingered on the brambles would make a good snack.

A few birds flitted around, but everything else rested quiet, including the breeze. I sat on the throne-like rock, settling back against the cool stone, resting my eyes, and allowing the stillness of the hill to slowly ease the tension from my mind.

No bear-like growls or grunts sounded, nothing even similar to the noises Flynn had warned me about.

Complete silence. Peace.

Humming sounded before I realized I'd begun, and I continued, singing the words in my mind rather than allow them to escape my mouth. The song Flynn's Ma had sung to him. The song that had drawn him to me, the song that had gifted me my first true kiss, the kind that swept a woman's heart up in hope, the brushing of lips that tingled toes.

I didn't doubt I loved Flynn. His calming spirit, the life-giving energy that flowed off him, lighting me up from the inside out.

Free to let it flow, I smiled while humming, not needing to hide what I felt, what I wanted—even if he didn't.

So what to do?

My song ended, and I opened my eyes, peaceful as the lazing white clouds in the high expanse of blue overhead.

I'd felt like something had called me to the hill...but what? And why?

Lifting my head to peer across the land below, I set my left arm on the stacked rocks fashioned to match the natural rest on my right. The rocks shifted beneath my light touch even though I'd settled my arm there plenty of times without a hint of movement on their part.

They'd been fitted together carefully, stacked in such a way they hadn't wobbled before—

A Steller Jay squawked to my right, jacking my heart rate, jerking me to my left with a shriek—and the arm rest toppled to the ground.

"Damn bird!" I half-laughed at him, hand to my heart as he let out another squawk.

He took to the sky, leaving me a shaking mess.

My focus darted around the brambles, adrenaline pumping my blood way too fast. Nothing stirred, and I let out a slow exhale, trying to calm the thump in my chest.

The arm rest...

The four flat rocks lay on the ground—and where they'd rested sat a cavity in the rock seat, a bundle of sorts nestled in its shallow depth.

Oiled parchment wrapped around a cloth bag...a leather-bound book inside.

Tiny letters lined the first page, but the date told me who the book belonged to. It'd been dated nineteen years earlier, and she'd only just arrived at the homestead.

Flynn's Ma.

Callan's first wife.

I glanced up, nervous that my having found her journal would bring the two men running, but peaceful silence still reined around me.

Returning my attention on the book laying open in my lap, I smoothed my fingers over the penciled words.

Her first day on the homestead had played out so closely to mine that my throat tightened. Callan had shown a side of him she hadn't seen before. He wasn't the man she'd known back in California mere weeks earlier, the seemingly respectful man who'd talked her into running away with him.

Tales of panning for gold and riches untold.

Promises of a picket fence, a walk-in closet, and a dozen children to fill the home he would build for her.

I clutched the journal to my chest, tears once more filling my eyes.

Two days. I had two, possibly three, to finish reading what had happened, why Flynn's Ma had felt the need to hide her journal away.

Hurrying down the hill, I remembered the drawing she'd done of Flynn sitting on that rock.

I expected she'd done it in hopes he would find what I held in my hands. While it would surely prove private, something had led me to that seat. The jay had squawked for seemingly no reason, revealing the journal's hiding spot.

A gift from a woman I expected would share in my misery from beyond the grave.

25

FLYNN

Pa decided to tell me all about his and Saige's sex life since I didn't sleep in the cabin to hear it for myself. If he hoped to make me jealous, create an urge in me to take myself in hand, he failed.

Tuning him out didn't work, and after his second night by the fire of putting into words how good her soft flesh felt under his hands, how easily her skin bruised beneath his fingertips, I'd reached my limit.

"Don't need to hear about your marriage bed, Pa," I stated through grit teeth while tossing Dog one of the hare bones from dinner that curdled in my stomach thanks to Pa's tales.

"Just trying to sway your mind the pussy way since you're a faggot, boy."

"I'm not a faggot."

"You're not, huh?"

I could feel Pa's dark gaze on me, but I busied myself stirring the fire's coals to add a few pieces to see us through the night.

"Well, if you're no faggot, that means you want pussy. Been thinking about Saige's?"

"No," I answered sharply—a bit too quickly, too. Lips snapping shut, I forced a slow inhale, telling myself to calm down, get my damn mind off how good that pussy had felt around my cock.

"Now why don't I believe you?"

"She's yours," I said. My nostrils flared even though I managed to keep my tone steady. "Just like the cabin, the canoe, the land...I'll have my own someday."

And maybe I'll have Saige, too. Somehow. Some way.

He chuckled, his voice dry from the tobacco he lit in his pipe. Sweet, sickly smoke curled in the air, and I moved to the other side of the fire, upwind from him.

"Lots of sign of beaver," I mentioned where we'd scouted earlier in the day, trying for casual, anything to get his mind off me and the woman I coveted. Craved.

"Beaver's another name for pussy."

I nodded, jaw once more clenched.

"You wouldn't want Saige's anyway," Pa said, shifting to get comfortable on the ground. He grunted and let out a loud fart. "She's a young thing like you, but dry as fuck."

She hadn't been dry for me—quite the opposite. Wet and slick... My cock twitched at the memory of her body sucking me in, and I rolled onto my side, Dog settling in beside me.

Maybe if you took an interest in her, what she wanted, what she liked and needed to get turned on, she'd be a little more ready for your rutting.

I kept the thought inside even though I knew it to be truth. While I might not know much about sex and relationships, it seemed obvious she'd been ready for me—but she'd been ready for him a time or ten, thinking back. I remembered the wet sounds of their fucking. Her soft whimpers of enjoyment. Had she wanted him then?

Why did I doubt that, especially when it'd happened after that day he'd made her cry, the day we'd finished the chicken coop?

She'd been thinking of me.

I clenched my eyes shut as the thought flared to life, biting back a groan. Bad enough I'd fucked my Pa's wife, but wondering over if she thought of me while he took her—maybe to make her life less miserable...

Desire for her, hot and heavy, swelled me, and the second Pa started snoring, I worked my length until shooting off in silence, burying my spunk beneath last year's leaf litter.

———

We got home the next afternoon, rain pounding down on us since early morning, and Saige's glances Pa's way setting my mind to wondering. I watched her more than usual, thinking over why she studied Pa so intently when he got preoccupied with eating dinner.

I couldn't read her face, but my stomach clenched at the thought she might actually be happy to see him—she didn't once look my way.

Pa ambled out to the outhouse not long after dinner, closing himself in from the rain that continued to dump like buckets. My heart beat heavier in my chest at the chance to speak to her alone.

"Saige."

She turned from doing the dishes, glancing at me where I sat on the edge of my bed.

"You okay?"

"Mmm." She nodded, her gaze flitting off my face quick as it landed there.

"Did you enjoy your quiet time?"

"I watched the sunrise and sunset both days you were gone," she murmured, her voice soft. "In peace and quiet."

"Sounds like a good time to me."

A soft smile curved her lip, but I could only see half from the profile she offered while bending over the dishes once more.

Leaning forward, I propped my elbows on my knees. "You seemed happy to see Pa."

I'd expected anything but the snort which she let out, easing my mind immediately.

"Happy to see *me*?" I asked when she didn't speak.

Again, she didn't answer.

"I was wrong, Saige," I told her, keeping quiet in case Pa returned faster than his usual after dinner shit. "Shouldn't have sent you away like I did the other night. I'm sorry."

Saige finally gave me her attention, turning so I could clearly see her big brown eyes in the lamp's light, watch the pulse beat in her neck.

"Wanting you isn't right, but I can't *not* think about you that way," I told her. "Can't keep thoughts of having you under me from filling my brain, tempting me to do unthinkable things."

"Like what?" she whispered, leaving her lips parted, a sight I couldn't look away from.

"Wanting you for my own. Making you my own."

"Flynn." She bit her lower lip, and I slid my gaze down over her shirt, her hardened nipples making my mouth water for another taste.

"I want to worship every inch of your skin. Lick and

nibble. Bury my nose between your thighs again, taste your need for me."

She gulped, and I found myself on my feet, ready to stride across the cabin and do just that.

The door latch jiggled, and I spun away, picking up the stack of images Saige had left atop my bed.

Me sitting on Ma's rock, Dog at my feet.

My cock ached, and I stayed put until I could hide it enough to escape into the woodshed.

26

SAIGE

An hour or so after Callan slept, I stared at the wall. Everything I'd learned about him, his past, ate at my stomach. Empathy should have swayed my heart toward him, but he'd caused too much damage with his words and actions. While I'd always thought of myself as a forgiving person, I couldn't find it in myself to forgive him for what he'd done to Joc, the way he spoke to both me and Flynn—even if his life prior to living in the wilderness had shaped him into the bastard he'd become.

There's no excuse for his behavior.

I'd denied him my body earlier that night, and my face still stung from where he'd slapped me. At least he hadn't forced me to spread my legs, which I'd expected. Perhaps not completely evil, but pretty damn close.

Did Flynn know the truth of his father? Is that why he put up with the manipulation, the teasing, and god-awful words spewed from his lips? Had he known about his mother's journal?

It didn't look like it'd been touched in its rock hiding spot for years on end, but I couldn't tell for sure if it'd been touched between the last time she'd put it there and two days earlier when I'd found it.

A tale of heartache, but also one where she'd found joy. In her little wildling. Her red-headed son who ran barefoot on the homestead, more interested in digging in the dirt, climbing trees, and chasing animals than behaving like a human child.

She'd been nothing short of a poet, creating images in my mind with her words, vibrant and emotional. I'd cried while reading. Laughed.

And found myself loving Flynn even more.

He had been the light of her life, her final days before becoming bedridden had focused on him and his love for her.

My heart ached to know such emotion. To have a child of my own, to give it all the attention and love denied me by my parents. Throat tight, I squeezed my eyes shut, willing away the tears.

Did Flynn feel the same way as I did? Did he long to experience the attention and affection his mother had lavished on him according to her own words? She'd stated her touch always soothed him. Melted him against her, no matter his anger or tears.

Callan let out a snort of a snore, furrowing my brow.

He had his reasons for being an asshole, but that didn't sway me toward thinking good of him.

We'd only been together a few long months, but more than enough time for his true nature to shine through the front he'd put on for me back in town. I'd been manipulated into becoming nothing more than a sex slave, a servant to care for his cabin.

Same as his first wife, and same as his first wife, I reaped the consequences.

And he repaid me by taking away my only friend.

But Flynn...

Warmth slowly seeped through my body, bringing my aching heart back to life. What more would he have confessed to if Callan hadn't returned from the outhouse when he had? Would he have taken advantage of my inability to say no to him? Would he have asked me to come to him again once Callan slept?

The moment had been stolen from us—but I decided to steal another one for myself.

I couldn't argue with the need, the love growing inside me, swaying me Flynn's way.

I slipped from bed, a steady leak of adrenaline into my system, thumping my heart in my chest. With little more than a whisper of my feet on the plank floor, I crept through the cabin, my way easily lit by the summer's night that never fully darkened.

Wind rustled over my night shirt as I slipped outside once pulling on my boots, carefully clicking the door shut behind me. Standing on the stoop, I studied the woodshed, thankful the rain had stopped. A shiver slid down my spine, lifting the hairs on my nape and arms.

I no longer believed wanting love, wanting Flynn was wrong. Callan's the one who'd created the wrong, and it served him right that his actions pushed me into his son's arms.

But I didn't go to Flynn to get revenge on his father. My booted feet carried me over the muddy earth toward the one who brought sunlight to my life. The song in my heart. He held the affection I craved, he wanted what I did.

Us.

Together.

He sat on his pallet in the woodshed as though waiting

for me, and I shoved off my boots and went to him without a word, pushing my night shirt up and over my head on my way.

Already breathing heavy, I straddled his lap, hating his pants kept me from becoming one with him immediately.

Our mouths came together in a rush, our moans mingling in my ringing ears.

Life.

A shuddering sigh rippled over me as he cradled my face, his thumbs tenderly sliding over my jawline, his tongue mimicking what I wanted, what I needed.

"Flynn," I choked out, grasping at his shoulders, desperation quaking my belly, shivering my skin.

He shifted, reaching between us to undo his pants, and without taking my mouth from his, I rose to my knees, giving him better access.

The hard heat of him slapped against my core as he shoved his pants down, and I gasped a soft cry, my fingers tangling in his longer hair falling from the tie he held it back with.

His hands grasped my waist, and I lowered, rubbing my wetness against his heated flesh. "Saige," he groaned, once more taking my mouth, his hips pushing upward, running the back of his cock through my slick core. "You want me."

"Always."

I shifted, grasped his base, and held his gaze while slowly sinking down over his thickness, working my hips to fit him deep inside me.

Once fully seated, I stilled, our breaths heavy in the dimness, the scent of sex musking the air around us.

"You're mine, Saige." Flynn brushed my hair from my face and sliding one hand around my back, pulling me tight against his hard chest. "Mine."

"Yes," I whispered against his lips, and we both moved, seeking release, every shift of my hips, every upward thrust of his swelling so much emotion inside me, tears leaked down my cheeks.

He lapped them away, his soft groans pulsing my inner walls around him. "I want to fill you up with my seed, Saige. So damn much...so fuckin' full."

I whimpered in agreement, and in one swift move, I lay on my back, my legs wrapping around his backside.

Flynn thrusted deep, and I cried out before he could capture my mouth. He rutted into me like an animal, eating at my lips and tongue, caging me beneath him with arms of steel.

I'd never felt more secure. More cherished.

His pelvis ground against my clit and I panted, hovering on the edge of ecstasy he'd given me before. "Flynn..."

"I know, Saige. I know." He reached between our sweating bodies, his fingers finding my throbbing nub as he backed off, dragging his long length from my core.

I bowed beneath him, and he shoved in, his calloused thumb pressing against me.

My body came undone, wetness gushing around his thrusting length, cries ripping from my lips.

He groaned my name, and wet heat burst deep inside me, his cock jerking, filling me exactly as he'd wanted.

Yes...

Gasping for breath, I clung to him, loving how my heart beat like it wanted to explode from my chest.

One last grunt, and he collapsed against me, hard, hot, and sweaty. Delicious. The whiskers against my neck pebbled my skin with goosebumps, but I soaked in the affection rather than shy away from the slight tickle.

"We should leave this place," I whispered into the night when my breath returned.

Flynn shifted slightly, but didn't lift fully off me, his cock still buried inside, keeping his cum in its proper place.

"I have no way to support you. Nothing of my own." Flynn sighed against my neck and kissed up to suckle on my ear lobe.

"I would be content living in a cave if it meant I could be with you."

He lifted onto his elbows, peering down at me in the dim light.

"I'm going to find a way, Saige."

My heart leaped along with the corners of my lips. "You want me."

"Always." He peppered my face with soft kisses, and the happiness inside me swelled with giggles.

"Fuckin' love to hear you laugh." Flynn planked, grinding his hips, smearing our combined cum all over our groins. "Love this, too. Wet—for me."

"Only you."

He continued his shallow movements, his cock thickening fully again. "You like having my cock shoved up your tight pussy, don't you?"

Oh God. His words sent a shot of arousal straight to my clit and heated my cheeks. "Yes."

He dragged out, hovering with only the thick head of him notched inside me. "Slow and easy?" A gentle nudge rubbed him along my walls, and I grasped at his arms, wanting him to cover me again with his hard muscle and soft skin.

"Yes."

Another withdraw, and I whimpered, digging my fingernails into him as he sank home once more.

"I want to touch you whenever I want," Flynn gritted out as though through clenched teeth. "So good," he groaned, brushing his nose over mine. "So fuckin' good." A swivel of his hips rubbed his pelvis against my clit, and I wiggled beneath him.

"Please..."

"Want more?"

"Yes," I panted against his lips.

A quick thrust jammed him against my cervix, and I gasped. "Harder?"

"Ungh," I groaned, head tipping back and eyes closing as he repeated the movement.

"Deeper?"

"God, yes."

Flynn pulled out and slammed back in, shoving my body along his blankets.

"Oh, fuck, Flynn."

He made a low noise in his throat. "Say that again."

"Fuck."

Smashing his mouth to mine, he stole my breath—and every single thought in my head.

———

Hours later, I carried his promise to figure out a way for us to be together, my heart light as my footsteps.

We'd fucked hard and fast.

We'd made love a second time.

The soreness between my thighs, the sting of having him inside me for half the night, curved my lips upward. I'd never felt more beautiful in my skin. He'd worshiped every inch, licking and kissing. Nibbling and whispering how perfect I was—perfect for him.

Eventually, I ended up in his arms, cradled in warmth.

Still smiling, I slipped into the silent cabin.

Silent.

My smile faded.

"Where the fuck you been?" Callan called from the bedroom.

Swallowing against the fear wanting to choke me, I shuffled across the main room. "Outhouse," I whispered once I reached our bedroom, thankful he hadn't lit a lamp to see my heated face.

"Been gone a long fucking time."

"Supper didn't agree with my stomach." I forced myself to crawl beneath the blankets, curling on my side to keep as far from him as possible.

"That so?"

"Mmm." Eyes clenched shut, I focused on breathing steadily, praying the frantic thump in my chest didn't shake the bed.

"Think you're lying." He wrenched my thighs apart with his leg and yanked my night shirt up.

"Callan, d-don't."

He pressed my face into the pillow and shoved two fingers between my thighs. "The fuck is this, wife?" Wet sucking sounds filled my ears as he rammed his fingers into me a few times, and I whimpered, panic rising to tighten my chest over the wetness left behind by his son. "Feels like cum to me."

His fingers disappeared—and he sniffed. "Smells like it too."

Wet sucking noises.

Oh God. I clenched my eyes shut.

"Tastes too salty to be yours alone," he whispered hotly against my ear.

"C-Callan—"

He grasped my hair and jerked me roughly up onto my knees.

I cried out, clawing at his fingers, tangling tight against my scalp.

"Been fucking my boy, haven't you?"

"No!" I shrieked, sure he ripped my hair from my head. "P-please, Callan! L-let me go!"

"You're *my* fucking wife. *Mine.*" He shoved me away from him, and I flew off the bed, landing hard on my hip.

I scurried on hands and knees, desperate to get to the door—escape him. Escape what his first wife had endured time and again.

Callan stalked after me, and one thrust of his foot slammed into my thigh and sent me tumbling. "You cheating whore!" he hollered, reaching for me. "I'll make you pay for this..."

I screamed, clawing at his face, kicking as we grappled on the plank flooring. "Flynn!" I shrieked, sobs ripping from me at the first fist shooting stars through my vision.

"*My* wife!"

"F-Flynn," I whimpered, trying to roll away as dizziness rolled over me. Darkness beckoned in my periphery... Escape.

27

FLYNN

I'd watched Saige shut herself into the cabin, and waited at the woodshed's door, breath held, same as I'd done the first time she'd come to me. My stomach in knots, I strained my ears...

She shrieked my name, and I took off across the yard, my heart pounding faster than my feet hitting the ground.

Dog sprinted at my side.

A shoulder to the door crashed it against the wall.

Saige lay limp beneath Pa, arms sprayed to her sides.

Pa held her neck in his hands, keening curses, shaking her hard enough her head bounced off the floor. "You'll pay for wanting my son! Calling for my son—you're *mine!*" Spittle flew from his lips, and rage, hot and raw, lit a fire inside me.

A roar bellowed from my chest, and I threw myself forward, ramming into Pa. We sprawled in a tumble, crashing into my bedstead. No thought filled my mind, merely the need to avenge. Give back what he'd dished out through the years.

I'd made a promise, one I would keep no matter whose blood shed—

His punishments needed to end.

My fists slammed into Pa, but he bucked me off.

"Enjoy my pussy, faggot?" He spat a glob of blood onto the floor.

Past the ability to speak, I ignored him, and both of us growling like feral animals. We came together again, fists hitting flesh. Grunts ripped from both our lungs.

"She's my wife," he bit out a few times, cursing with every hit I landed.

She's mine to protect, my head argued, but my mouth couldn't form the words. Instead, I showed him with my fists. My knees. My elbows.

One hard hook from him sent pain radiating through my side, and I stumbled in a daze.

Pa came at me—and Dog leaped without a sound, his teeth going for the jugular. Dog hit Pa hard, jaw snapping in other-worldly silence. No growls, no barks. His teeth sank into Pa's forearm, and Pa swung around, ripping Dog from his flesh, and sending him smashing against the wall.

The loud crack tore through the heaviness of the cabin, and I knew without watching Dog slump to a heap on the floor that his chest would never rise again, that his days of hunting hare alongside me had ended.

Dog.

Throat tight, my eyes burning, I gave over to the blood-thirsty rage swelling inside me. Pa had killed my best friend. He would not beat me. He would not touch Saige again— my lover. My entire fuckin' world.

She's all I had left.

I would be strong enough for her. I would provide for

her—starting by giving her the freedom she needed in order to be mine.

I barreled forward and threw my shoulder into Pa's chest, sending him backward, both of us crashing onto the table. It collapsed beneath us, jarring Pa enough he didn't bring his arms up to block my fists I rained down on his face.

"Killed Dog!" I screamed down at him, tears and blood running from my nose with abandon as I smashed my knuckles into him over and over. "Hurt Ma!"

Blood sprayed from his nose.

"No! More!" I managed the words between my fists, landing against his flattened nose.

"F-Flynn."

My raised arm paused at the soft call, and I blinked twice before finding my focus beyond the need to drive Pa's head into the ground.

Saige.

She pushed up onto her haunches, one hand clutching Dog's fur.

I glanced back down at Pa to find his mouth slack, eyes closed.

Knocked out cold.

Biting back a sob, I shot out a last fist to his temple, and climbed off him, wiping my forearm across my bleeding nose.

"Are you alright?" I pulled Saige up off the floor into my arms, searching her face.

"I-I think so."

A mark darkened her cheek.

"He hit you?"

She gently touched my cheek, but I didn't feel a damn thing from the adrenaline still coursing through me. "Yes."

My jaw clenched as I smashed down my heartache, but I stayed put rather than turn to finish what I'd started. I'd spilled blood, but...

Ma.

"Think you can walk a bit?" I rasped out.

"Mmm hmm."

A quick glance at Pa revealed he hadn't moved other than the rise and fall of his chest. "Pack your stuff," I told Saige. "We're leaving."

I lit a lamp and kept an eye on Pa while we stuffed our packs full, neither of us speaking—hurrying to be gone before he woke and things got ugly again. While Saige dressed, I quickly tossed some food into a sack.

At Pa's lack of movement, I wondered if I'd caused permanent damage. Would serve the bastard right.

So would a bullet to his brain.

I toyed with the thought while checking my rifle, considered keeping my promise that if he'd ever hurt Saige I would kill him, but my promise to Ma trumped the desire to bury him.

I hadn't been strong enough for Saige... Anger kept other emotion at bay as I scurried to pack enough things to see us through a week or so.

Lighting out like I planned, we wouldn't have time to bury Dog. Jaw clenched, I eyed him laying beneath the window overlooking the river. He'd been my life, my best friend for so damn long...

And now I have Saige.

"You're a good boy," I whispered, fingers clenched to keep from scratching under his chin.

"Ready." Saige moved toward me, her hair a tangled mess, eyes wide and frightened, and the need to protect her, love her, flooded through me, ripping my thoughts off my grief over Dog.

I stuffed two boxes of rifle shells into my pack and slung it over my arms to settle on my back. Grabbing up my rifle and the food sack, I eyed her jeans, sturdy boots, the t-shirt stretched tight over her bra-less chest peeking from her unzipped sweatshirt. She, too, had slung her pack over her back. "I'm going to take care of you," I vowed, keeping my voice void of the emotions battering my insides.

She nodded, tears welling in her eyes, keeping my thoughts focused on what needed done.

Without another word, we walked out into the night, river-bound.

28

SAIGE

Somehow, I bottled up my frayed emotions and focused on putting one foot in front of the other as Flynn clasped my hand in his and led me down to the rushing river. Neither of us spoke, not that I would have found words.

My head ached, my cheek smarted, and my heart beat heavy in my chest as the adrenaline slowly ebbed from my bloodstream. Shivers wracked through me, and I clenched my jaw to keep my teeth from chattering.

Cool breezes stirred my hair, our quick footfalls crunching the pebbles lining the path.

Flynn dragged the canoe closer to the water, one end bobbing as he held it steady. "In."

I obeyed, my shaking hands grasping at the sides while trying to settle facing away from him. A shrug of my shoulders slid my pack off my back and onto the canoe's bottom between our seats.

Flynn dropped his bag and the food goods alongside mine, shoved the canoe, and hopped on, rocking us into the swift current.

I had no idea where we were headed, what he planned, but I trusted him to have our best interest in heart. Perhaps civilization lay a few days south of us—but I didn't have the energy or brain power to talk details.

Escape. The only word I could focus on without losing my shit.

The paddle dipped into the water behind me, and I sat hunched, shivering. Fighting off a deep-boned chill.

Damnitalltohell, I'd made one hell of a mistake heading out into the wilderness with a man I'd hardly known. Caught up in manipulation, grasping at lies, hoping to find something better.

I found something better.

The memory of Flynn's caresses overshadowed the ache in my cheek, in my head. Clinging to thoughts of him eventually filled me with warmth enough my shivering stopped.

"Where are we going?" I finally asked, my eyes scratchy as my voice.

"Jessie's husband, Brock, has a cabin a little ways downriver."

"How far?" I asked, exhaustion drooping my shoulders.

"Two days' hike, but with the river running like this, won't take as long. Tired?"

"Exhausted."

"You can lie down here in the canoe's bottom and rest."

The thought of rest, of lying down, closing my eyes, and escaping stung my eyes with tears.

"Go on, Saige."

Having better control over my muscles made shifting around and getting into the bottom of the canoe easier than climbing in had been. I nestled my feet between Flynn's and used my backpack as a pillow.

"Close your eyes and rest."

I let out a heavy exhale and did as told, the gentle rock of the water as Flynn steered us southward quickly lulling me to sleep.

———

Cold water splashed my face, jarring me awake to full daylight. The canoe rocked, and I scrambled to sit, hands grasping the sides.

Flynn's pale face set, quickly glancing at me before focusing on the paddle in his hands, and angling it in the swift water.

"Hold still and hang on." His low tone hinted at concern, as did the furrow on his brow.

I glanced over my shoulder to find more rapids ahead of us. Big ones—big rocks, too.

Oh god.

The need to turn fully, to face where we headed screamed in my brain, but I forced myself to hold still as Flynn had said. Shifting and rocking the canoe beneath my scrambling around would only make his job harder.

We dipped into a swell, cold river water splashing up to slash at my face and fall into the canoe's bottom.

Turning back around toward Flynn, I clutched at the canoe's sides—and kept my focus on him. Tense shoulders rippled beneath his shirt as he shifted the oar from side to side, digging into the water. Back paddling. Steering us through the dips and rises of the river caused by unseen rocks and those quickly passing in a blur of brown, green, and blue in my periphery.

Shallow breaths eventually starved my lungs, and I

forced myself to inhale deeper. Let it eek out. The shivers started back up, the occasional splash of river water over the canoe's sides chilling me through.

A good two or so inches sat in the canoe's bottom with me, soaking my pants and underwear, but I didn't get up— kept my focus on Flynn's face.

"Hang on!" He spat out through clenched teeth, whipping the oar to his left, muscles straining in his neck as he shoved it down and held it deep in the water.

The canoe bucked beneath us, lifting my backside clear off the bottom.

I shrieked, clutching at the sides. "Flynn!"

He swung the oar to his other side, straight out—and it snapped as he shoved it against a huge rock.

We careened sideways.

"Saige!"

Our eyes met and held.

My breath stalled.

A heartbeat, and we tipped. Water swallowed me, muting the sound of his hollering my name again.

Cold closed over me, stealing my breath.

Lashing, tugging—water pulled on me, sweeping me up in a current I couldn't fight. Kicking and fighting didn't bring my head above water.

I slammed into something, and I fought to keep from an instinctive inhale.

My head broke the water, and I gasped, filling my lungs. "Flynn!"

"Saige!"

Water filled my ears again as I swirled downstream, muffled gurgles of water drowning out the sobs building in my chest.

Another break for air, another shriek of his name.

The water yanked me beneath the surface again. Another slam against a rock brought whimpers to my lips, and I reached out with my fingers, grasping at nothing but water—empty and helpless.

Flynn...

29

FLYNN

Hiking downriver would have been safer with the rain we'd had, but the canoe promised to get us away from Pa faster and without leaving tracks. Once he woke up —if he ever did—he would find the canoe gone and figure out where we headed.

At least we would have a full two days before he'd catch up to us.

The second I lost control in the river, however, I realized I'd made a mistake. I'd kept my promise to Saige, but I dumped her into the river, and the helplessness of losing her to the rushing water knifed through my chest.

"Saige!" I screamed again while fighting the current, catching sight of her hair swirling away, too damn far. I swam hard, the water pushing at my back, but she remained out of reach, the angry current whipping her away from me.

"Saige!"

She banged against a rock and quit flailing.

No!

The rapids eased up seconds later, and I managed to grab a handful of her hair, a quick tug pulling her back against my chest. Flipping onto my back and kicking, I held us both above water.

"Stay with me, Saige—I got you."

She lay limp in my arms, complete dead weight, but as the river once more flattened around us, I got us to land.

Her chest rose and fell in a steady rhythm as I pulled her up onto the pebbled shore, and a nice goose egg swelled the side of her head, but she didn't bleed.

"Sorry. So damn sorry. Should have stayed on land," I told her, carefully checking her head, my throat tight, and chest still aching. "Knew it was dangerous with all this rain we had. Stupid. Stupid!"

The canoe lay capsized a ways downriver, but I didn't catch sight of our packs.

"It's going to be okay. I'll take care of you." I kissed her forehead, the warmth of her skin giving me hope. "Promise."

Fire. Shelter. My mind went straight toward the first things needed for survival, and I carried Saige a ways from the water, finding a mossy area to camp out until she woke.

Luckily, I kept my flint in my pocket, and my knife attached to my side. A bit of dried moss and twigs got a flame going, and I fed the fire steadily, ever watchful over Saige whose pale cheeks worried me.

We'd gone down river far enough I knew Pa wouldn't catch a whiff of our fire, so I curled up behind my woman, kept her back warm while the fire dried out her front. My eyelids grew heavy from the lack of sleep in the previous twenty-four hours, and I allowed myself to relax, knowing we didn't face any immediate danger.

———

Saige shifted in my arms, pulling me from a deep sleep. My eyelids snapped open, and I smoothed her hair back, burying my nose in the dried strands.

"Saige?"

"Hmm?"

Relief shot through me at her murmur. "Are you okay?"

"Mmm." She stretched and let out a small groan. "My head hurts. What happened?"

"You bashed up against a rock."

"And you saved me."

"Of course."

Saige let out a sigh and snuggled back against me. Damp clothes lay between us, but I felt down over her front to find her shirt dried out by the fire that had died down to embers.

"Cold?"

"No," she whispered, lacing her fingers through mine atop her belly.

My cock swelled against the crack of her backside, her scent filling my nose, but I held still. "There's an old radio at Brock and Jessie's—or at least there was one last time I was there with Pa. I'm going to have Jessie come get you."

Saige rolled, her big brown eyes studying my face, a slight frown denting her smooth skin. "You don't want me?"

"Fuck, yes, I want you." I pulled her tighter against me, resting my forehead against hers. "But I want you safe. Far away from Pa. You need to get your head checked out." I gently ran my fingertips over the bump, pleased to feel it hadn't swollen any bigger.

"I feel fine, Flynn," she murmured, clutching at my shirt. "Please don't send me away."

A heavy weight I hadn't realized attached itself to my chest slid away, air sliding easily into my lungs. I let out a shuddered exhale. "Last thing I want is you gone."

"Then let me stay with you."

Our noses brushed a few times, and I took her lips in a sweet kiss even though it made my cock leak with the need to be inside her warm body.

"Not leaving you," she whispered against my lips, sliding her leg over my hip.

I groaned, grabbed her fleshy backside, and gave into the need to grind my aching length against her. Our kiss turned greedy, tongues and heated breath—but I pulled back before instinct had me ripping her pants off.

"There's plenty of daylight left—we need to get going."

"Five minutes."

Another groan rolled from my chest. "There's a bed at Brock's. Food. I'll feel ten times better having a roof over your head and a door to barricade just in case."

Saige stared at my lips, her fingertips running over my beard. "You think he'll come after us." She didn't ask a question, but I would not lie or hide the truth.

"Yes. It's only a matter of time."

"Is it awful of me to hope he bleeds out instead?"

My fists had caused damage to his face, no doubt, but not enough of his life's blood would drain to stop his heart. The thought I should have ended him slid through my brain, and I worried over my cold-hearted reaction. I could have done it without emotion.

Should have.

"It's not awful," I stated gruffly, cradling her face in my hands. "Part of me wishes I'd ended his miserable life right there on the cabin floor. The way he hurt Ma...the way he hurt you." My stomach clenched up tight along with my lips before I started sharing the things closest to my heart.

"Thank you." Saige's soft whisper and the tears welling in her eyes gave me something other than anger to focus on.

"I would do anything for you, Saige."

She leaned in and pressed her lips to mine, lingering and licking—I know what she wanted, the same as me, but her safety came before my need for her body.

"We have to go."

Her sweet breath caressed my mouth on a sigh. "Okay."

She sat, denying pain even though her face flinched from the movement. Once on her feet, she let out a heavy exhale and nodded. "I'm good."

I took a few more seconds to study her face, her eyes— she seemed to be telling me the truth. But I kept her hand firmly clasped in mine while kicking out the embers and heading downriver to salvage what I could find of our belongings.

30

SAIGE

We found my backpack not far from the canoe which had cracked across the hull, but no trace of Flynn's or the food sack. His rifle had also disappeared, probably resting at the river's bottom.

My head and my face where Callan had hit me throbbed, but I fought to hide my pain, not wanting to worry Flynn more than he already was.

His head kept on the move, swiveling to watch around us, sometimes halting us for a few moments to stand and listen.

I clung to his hand, needing the warmth, the solid feel of him to keep me grounded. My mind ran amok, quickly exhausting me over thoughts of mistakes I'd made, part of me not wanting to call them so because I'd met Flynn and cheated on my husband even though the asshole deserved to rot in hell. The lack of guilt even bothered me, and I wondered at the woman the wilderness had shaped me into in a matter of months.

Running on instinct and desire rather than morals.

Animalistic action rather than restraint.

"We'll have to sleep out here again tonight."

"Okay," I murmured, not caring where we spent the night as long as he lay beside me. Held me.

"Are you hungry?"

"I'll be fine." My stomach cramped in disagreement, but I wouldn't die of hunger before we got to Brock's cabin.

Flynn had told me while walking along the river that Jessie offered the use of the place at any time, telling him it sat stocked with goods to see a person through for a few weeks. While we wouldn't have a gun, we would survive.

But for how long, and for *what*, we didn't discuss.

Between the two of us, we had nothing, no means of creating a life. The memory of that shroud of darkness whenever Callan had come close to me raised the hairs on my arms, and the sudden desire to be without that sense, that feeling of danger, rose quick and harsh, tightening my throat.

Adrenaline shot into my blood stream, and within seconds my knees grew weak and breaths shortened.

I wanted the dread gone. I wanted to be free of it —of him.

We could radio Jessie. Have her pick us up, and I would find a way to repay her. I would file for divorce. Free myself from Callan, free myself for Flynn, and we could live happily ever after.

I felt sure I could get my old job back, even if it meant standing and listening to my co-worker bitch for hours on end. If Flynn waited for me at home, nothing would bother me, nothing would sag my shoulders with depression like life used to do.

But what if Flynn didn't want to leave the wilderness? He'd been born a wildling, his mother had stated—

Oh God.

"Flynn," I choked out his name, stumbling.

He grabbed me into his arms in a rush. "What is it? Are you okay?"

I stared up into his soft green eyes, my heart torn. Aching. I hadn't thought to grab his mother's journal from its hiding place in the rocks. In my selfish need to be with him, be under him, I hadn't even thought to tell him what I'd found, all I'd learned about her, his Pa...

"Your mother had a journal," I croaked out.

A frown flitted over his brow and smoothed out a second later. "Yes—I remember her writing whenever we went to pick berries." He focused on my eyes. "You found it."

I nodded, my throat tight and tears filling my eyes. "I-I didn't think to tell you. I was so caught up, and—"

He pressed a quick kiss to my lips. "It's okay."

"D-do you know...have you read it?"

"No."

I expected he had no clue who his father was, where he'd come from, the past that had dictated the man he'd become.

"It was buried beneath the rock arm rest on that stone seat up by the brambles."

A low chuckle rumbled his chest. "Of course, it was. Now that you say it, I remember seeing her rearranging those rocks every time she sat there."

"You're not mad I read it?"

"Not at all."

I closed my eyes and rested my forehead against his chest, breathing in the wild scents of nature clinging to him. If he knew what lay between those pages with the cramped words, he might think differently.

It's up to me to tell him.

"Your Pa..."

"Not now, Saige. Pa has no place between us." He kissed the top of my head, his tone guarded, almost hard while shutting me down. "Let's find a place to camp. Sleep. Let's focus on getting to Jessie and Brock's. Then we'll talk. We'll make a plan, okay?"

I pulled back, my heart swelling to near bursting at the emotion he allowed me to see in his eyes. "Okay."

————

We didn't reach the cabin until late the next afternoon. My head felt better, but my feet killed me. The grumbling of my stomach dented my forehead in a frown, and the second Flynn opened a can of stew, I told him I didn't care if it was cold. He handed it over, and I chowed down, not looking up until I finished.

He stared at me, a smirk on his lips, the opened can in front of him untouched.

"What?"

"I love to watch you eat."

I snorted, licking the back of my spoon.

"Seriously. That day..." His voice trailed off, his smile fading.

"Joc."

"Yeah, but even before then, you weren't eating."

"Depression will do that to a person." I glanced around Jessie and Brock's cabin, loving the simplicity, the single room, the tidy space with everything having a set spot. I could be content in such a place. Small, but who needed more?

"You've lost weight since you came out here."

I shrugged, inspecting the empty can for another taste.

Flynn slid his can over. "I'll grab another one." He

hopped up from the chair and turned, reaching for the shelving along the wall behind him. I still watched him when he sat.

"What?" he asked, one eyebrow raised.

"I love to watch you move."

His gaze darkened, and I knew I'd hit something good, delicious in his mind. "I love moving around you—in you."

"Oh God."

His low chuckle tingled me between the thighs, and I pressed them tight. "Finish eating, Saige."

I tore my focus off his mouth, my face heating.

He opened his can, and we ate in silence. The weight of what had happened, the overturned canoe that had cracked on a rock, the journey along the river fell over me.

Sitting back, I let out a heavy exhale and pushed the half-finished can toward Flynn. "I'm exhausted," I whispered as the truth settled into my bones.

"Why don't you take off your boots and go get comfortable?" He said, motioning toward the bed with his chin.

"Yeah." I sat, too tired to move for a few more minutes while he ate.

Without a word, he finished, picked me up, and carried me to the bed. He set me on the edge, bending to his knees to take off my boots.

We had dried out completely, but our little swim in the river had left our clothes stiff, the long walk dirtying them. The thought of needing to do laundry since we didn't have other clothing flitted through my brain, but Flynn pulled off my shirt.

"Lay back."

I did as told, and he stripped me of my pants.

"Under the covers you go."

He pulled the blankets back, and I snuggled beneath,

fighting to keep my eyes open to watch as he took off his boots and shed his clothes.

"Close your eyes. Let me hold you."

A shuddering sigh rippled through me, and I melted into his embrace. Warm skin. Hairy leg between mine, hot breath on the top of my head. My eyes closed on their own, and even though moisture sprang to life between my thighs at having him fully against me, nothing but my panties between us, exhaustion tugged me down.

I went willingly, more content than I'd ever been in my entire life.

31

FLYNN

I woke before Saige and slipped from the bed without waking her.

Nothing stirred outside from what I could see, but I'd locked us up tight inside Brock's cabin. No chance of man or animal getting inside. Poking around as quiet as possible to not to disturb Saige's much-needed sleep, I found Brock's old radio and a pistol. A box of shells eased my shoulders.

At least I had some means of protecting Saige beyond my knife if Pa found us before I could get in touch with Jessie.

I didn't want Saige to leave, but I couldn't ask her to stay with me when I had no way to feed, shelter, or protect her through the long months ahead.

Sitting naked at the table, I watched her sleep. Her soft lips parted, tempting me to kiss her awake, but the bruise on her cheek...

She'd learned something about Pa in Ma's journal, no doubt. But I hadn't wanted to hear it. Didn't want to think about him, didn't give two piles of bear shit about him. But did I want to hear Ma's written words? Did I want to learn her emotions, her thoughts? Did I want to hear about her crushed dreams, how much her life probably aligned with Saige's?

I remembered enough to know her life had been far from pleasant, and I knew my birth, my presence in her life had given her joy. She'd told me so countless times.

"Flynn," Saige whispered, lifting my focus off the worn floorboards where I hadn't realized it'd drifted.

"Good morning, beautiful."

Pink fused her cheeks as she blinked at me, and my cock woke up from the shit I'd been thinking on.

I stood, and her attention dropped to the hardening length I held in my hand. She lifted the covers back, offering me a place to lay—and I took it, sliding right on top of her and taking her mouth, morning breath be damned.

She cradled me between her thighs, her hands smoothing along my spine and back up, our mouths fused. Breaths shared. Our hearts beat in time between us, heightened with every swipe of our lips.

"Need you," she whispered, and I shifted, finding her wet heat smearing along the back of my cock. "Please—"

I pushed in, taking her mouth hard at the pure perfection of her stretching around me, sucking me in deeper. Fuckin' hell, her body had been made for mine.

"Saige," I groaned, bottomed out, deep as I could go.

"Yes."

Lower lip between my teeth, I planked on my elbows and ground against her, pulling little gasps from her mouth.

Big brown eyes stared up at me with such trust and... love, my heart ached.

"Never letting you go, Saige." I pulled out and slid back

in, flexing my ass, wishing I could go deeper inside her, clear through to her soul.

She clutched at my shoulders, wiggling her hips beneath me and whimpering.

"You're mine."

"Yes."

All I needed to know—I gave over to the instinct to mate, tasting and touching, trying to soak every second of our time together deep into my memory. Our bodies rose and fell together, in perfect rhythm, until she came around me, crying out my name.

I pressed my face into her neck and gave her all I had. Saige owned my body, and I handed over my heart along with it, hoping like hell we would find a way to make things work for us.

———

I brought in firewood, and we started up the wood stove to make coffee even though night fall wasn't too far off. More stew and green beans made up our dinner, and I sat on the bed, propped against the headboard at her insistence while she washed up dishes with the water I'd brought up from the river.

In nothing more than panties and a t-shirt, she tempted me to take her again. We had discussed nothing serious over dinner, but it was time for a good, long talk. Enjoying her body would have to wait.

When she finished, I patted the bed beside me. Saige curled up against me, her cheek on my chest, and I wrapped my arms around her, one hand working at the tangles in her hair.

"Tell me what you read in Ma's journal."

And she did. Everything she could remember, and I simply leaned my head back, eyes closed, forcing myself to stay calm as she recounted the events. Pa wasn't the man I'd always thought. Where he came from—his family.

My jaw ached from clenching it even as my heart thawed the slightest bit. Ma had always told me to try to see things from other people's perspective. Doing so gave me a better understanding of the man who'd raised me, but didn't reason away his treatment of me, or her.

No one deserves abuse, physical or emotional, and there's never any excuse for it, either.

Pa was still a bastard in my mind, but knowing him, what had formed him into a man, left me relieved I hadn't taken his life like I'd wanted to. Perhaps he died of blood loss, but it wasn't done intentionally by my hand like I'd been tempted to do.

"Are you okay?" Saige asked quietly when I didn't speak for some time after she quieted.

I rubbed along her arm, loving the soft feel of her skin beneath my hardened hands. "Yes."

She snuggled in closer, kissing my chest, her lips lingering. "I'm not leaving you, Flynn. Ever."

Hugging her tight, I fought off the thickness in my throat. "I love you," I managed to choke out.

Saige climbed onto my lap, my whiskered cheeks in her hands, her eyes wet even though a smile tilted her lips, letting me see that cute tooth. "Do you mean it?"

"Without a doubt. Forever. Always." I grasped her hips and tugged her tight against me.

"I love you, too." Her smile lit like the sun, warming me clear through to my toes.

One heated kiss later, I ripped off her panties, lifted her above my leaking length, and yanked her down.

Claiming.

Owning.

Pa and the whole world be damned.

32

SAIGE

Two full days of nothing but eating, sleeping, and being beneath Flynn. Pure heaven, the kind of life and love I'd hoped to find but never expected. Every time he entered my body, he held me close, looked into my eyes, whispered words of affirmation, drawing me in deeper, dousing me with his life-giving energy.

I smiled all day, every day.

Sometimes, I caught Flynn looking out over the river, his brow furrowed, but he would shake his head and tell me it was nothing when I asked what bothered him. He never used the radio to call for Jessie.

We lived in limbo, but the level of comfort I drew from Flynn didn't allow for fear or concern. I'd found what I'd been longing for, and no one or nothing would take it away from me.

If it meant living in a cave, I would gladly do so—as long as I had my love by my side.

He fished beside me at the river's edge while I washed out my panties. While a few articles of clothing had been left in the cabin, Jessie didn't have any feminine things. I wore her shirt and a pair of sweatpants, but both were a bit too small. Not that Flynn minded my thighs being snuggled inside the pants.

Brock and he were close in size, so the clothes he wore fit better.

He kept watch while fishing, his gaze always on the move, ever vigilant.

We walked to the cabin, hand-in-hand, my heart and steps light. Living in my own little world hadn't ever felt so right. An absolute dream.

The cabin door ahead offered our escape, its bed my favorite piece of furniture ever. Squeezing his hand, I glanced up to find his forehead dented with another frown.

"Are you okay?"

"Yeah."

I didn't trust his rumbled reply, a hint of doubt pinging through my chest, fading my smile. "I'll fry up these fish like I did with the ones last night. There's canned corn and those potatoes you like. I found a can of peaches too—your favorite. We'll dine like kings tonight." My voice faded off when his face didn't twitch.

A blast sounded, and Flynn jolted forward with a grunt, his hand ripping from mine, Brock's fishing pole he'd held clattering to the ground.

My brain didn't register—until blood poured down the side of his head as he fell, face first, inches from the stoop.

"Flynn!" I shrieked, realizing he'd been shot, the string of fish I'd held tossed aside in my haste to grab him up against me. "Flynn!"

His eyes rolled back into his head, and the blood...

Damnitalltohell.

"Stay with me, Flynn." I choked on a sob, grabbing him beneath his arms and tugging him up the stoop. He moved inch by inch with every tug, panicked sobs rising to choke me. Adrenaline allowed me to push in the door and get him partway up the steps before his boot got caught between two.

My heart slammed in my chest as I screamed and yanked, desperate to get him into our escape.

He's going to be fine. Just fine.

Cold darkness, the shroud I recognized, lifted the hairs on my body. Motion in my periphery caught my attention, and I jerked my head to the side, my arms going limp at the sight of Callan.

Purple bruises marred his face. Dried, crusted blood clung to his filthy shirt and matted hair. His pale eyes held so much more than the usual coldness.

Unstable.

Madness.

"Hello, there, *wife.*"

My heart stalled out, and although the instinctive need to survive tensed my muscles up tight to throw myself at him, scream and rage, claw his eyes out, I held myself still. "Callan," I whispered through the tears, the tightness in my throat as he moved closer. Memories of his past rushed through my head, and I knew I only had one chance to save Flynn, only one chance to survive. I'd learned in my time in the wilderness. I knew how to manipulate, to lie. "You hurt your s-son," I whispered, holding his gaze. "Your *only* son who has only ever wanted a k-kind word."

He pulled up short, the rifle's shoulder strap clanking as he shifted his hold on its stock and barrel.

"He n-needs help. Please, Callan." I sucked oxygen into my lungs, trying again to tug Flynn farther into the house.

Callan glanced down over his unmoving boy.

"He needs you, Callan," I whispered. "P-please. I-I'll do anything you want. Anything you say. Just call Jessie on the radio and I'll go back with you. We can return to our life on the homestead, just you and me. We can be happy together, the two of us. I won't ever leave you like she did. Won't ever let anything take your place in my heart." The bullshit poured from my lips in an attempt to sway him to do what I wanted, what I needed, in order to save the man I loved.

"He stole from me. Tried to take you away from me—same as he did *her.*"

"No!" I rushed to say, my head whipping back and forth while I swallowed. "No! It was all me, Callan. I-I went to him. I tempted him. What happened was all my fault."

He turned his cold eyes on me, the lack of empathy or emotion in them shivering my body.

"Please, Callan," I pleaded, my voice as broken as my heart. "Be the father you always wanted."

His whiskers twitched as though he clenched his jaw, the only sanity of life on his face. "Leave him."

"Not until you promise to radio J-Jessie."

Callan's gaze softened as he lifted his focus back to my face. "Okay." He set his gun on the ground and started toward me once more, but without the predatory gait of a man intent on causing harm.

Still, my muscles stayed tensed beneath me.

"Let me take a look." He started to crouch down beside us, and I glanced down at Flynn and the blood still leaking along the side of his head to soak my sweatpants.

Pain exploded across the side of my cheek, the smash of the doorjamb against the other side of my face.

He hit me...

I sagged back into the cabin, blinking up at the log

ceiling overhead, my heartbeat slowing along with my breath.

He'd lied—why had I believed him?

Callan's dark energy floated over me, along with the promise of disappearing to unconsciousness. He grabbed me by my hair, the sting along my scalp bringing a whimper to my lips and keeping me alert.

"You can't leave me, too," he muttered.

My arms like deadened limbs, I attempted to brush him off, twist away as he dragged me away from Flynn, from the stoop.

I thought I'd been smart. Strong enough to manipulate a man unmoved by emotion other than anger. Bitterness for all he'd endured as a child.

I hadn't been strong enough, but given another chance, I wouldn't fail.

Pebbles dug into me as he started off with steady strides, pulling me along behind him like slaughtered game, my backside and legs dragging on the ground.

Flynn lay unmoving in the cabin's open doorway...

Tears coursed down my cheeks, but I kept quiet. Held onto my conscience state, and when Callan finally released his hold on my hair and demanded I get on my feet, I found the strength.

Every step northward, cutting across land rather than following the river, I dragged my feet. Brushed against grasses, bushes, and anything else I could disturb in order to leave a trail Flynn could follow without having to look too closely.

If Flynn never woke, if I'd lost him forever, I wanted whoever found him to have a clear path to the one who'd hurt him—even if Callan didn't plan to let me live long enough to see him pay for what he'd done.

I would live. I would get revenge.

It was only a matter of time.

————

I expected Callan to force me onto my hands and knees so he could have what he felt belonged to him. Even though I'd pledged my life to him, he no longer deserved it—and I no longer felt he had the right to use my body for his own pleasure.

Callan left me sitting by the fire, watching me from its other side, his eyes cold even though the fire reflected off them. He'd bound my wrists and ankles, making escape impossible. Coolness descended as the sun lowered, and I shivered in my shirt, arms wrapped around my knees, sitting as close to the fire as possible.

Other than stare at me, Callan left me alone. Didn't speak. Didn't touch me. Perhaps the thought his son had been inside me sickened him enough he didn't feel the need to reclaim what he saw as his.

Or perhaps he waited until we returned to the homestead.

Either way, sorrow still shrouded over me like a wool blanket, heavy and suffocating. Had my love lived? Did he still breathe? The blood he'd lain in had seemed too much, but I clung to hope.

Callan had lived and come after us. I had to believe Flynn would do the same.

The second day I trudged northward behind Callan, the rope he'd used to bind my ankles the night before used like a leash.

Bound like a dog. Dragged behind its owner. Without free will.

I didn't bother trying to play on his emotions. The past that had shaped him into the man he'd become. Madness reined in his eyes. The type I knew I couldn't reason with. His own narcissistic father had hardened him past the point of empathy. Attempting to reason with him would only lead to more fists, more pain, more bruising.

Flynn's Ma had known that best and written her woes in cramped handwriting. I would learn from her mistakes. Keep my head lowered, my mouth quiet, until opportunity afforded me a chance at escape.

Jessie would fly in with supplies in a matter of weeks. I only needed to keep my own sanity and stay alive until that time.

I would find a way to speak with her. I would find a way of escape if Flynn never came for me. Jessie and Brock would take me to their cabin. We would find the truth of what happened to my love.

The second night, I sat bound by the fire once more, shoulders hunched against the chilly air. Callan sat wrapped in a coat, rifle over his knees. Even if the chance of hypothermia lay on my doorstep, I wouldn't have asked for him to share his warmth.

Closing my eyes, I shut out reality and thought on my time with Flynn. Of his arms around me, having him move inside me. His warm breath on my lips, the scent of the wilderness, of nature, clinging to his skin. Soft whiskers along my skin. Between my thighs.

I shivered, but not from the cold, but I bit back the smile wanting to tilt my lips at the life my memories brought back.

Flynn.

He lived. Had to. I couldn't survive thinking otherwise.

A low grunt beyond Callan jerked my eyelids up, and he hopped to his feet and spun, rifle in hands.

I held my breath, my heart rushing enough adrenaline through my blood to heat me through.

The sound I'd been told to listen for.

Bear.

The beast sounded its voice again, but farther to my right. Enough darkness had taken the night sky I couldn't see deeply into the surrounding trees. Logs in the fire cracked, shooting sparks upwards, but no other sound rose in my ears past the rapid thumps of my heart.

I let out an exhale, but only because my lungs starved for oxygen.

Shuffling noises jerked my head over my right shoulder. Whatever it was had circled around, moved closer—

Callan stood, his eyes wide. Crazy. "Get out of here!" he hollered, rifle trained toward where the noises had come from. "Go on! Get!"

I huddled in on myself, my heart ready to explode in my chest.

Another snort.

Callan hollered a manic shriek and shot wildly into the woods behind me.

My ears rang, the crack of the gun slowly fading without the rush of a bear coming in to claim us as his dinner. Had Callan hit the beast?

He stood still, eyes wild as the hair atop his head, gaze flickering back and forth beyond me as though he didn't know the bear's location. The rifle shook in his hands.

Silence descended, every crackle or pop from the fire shooting a fresh burst of adrenaline through me.

Snuffling rose from behind Callan, and he hollered obscenities, jerking around and shooting in one motion.

Empty woods swallowed the ringing crack from the rifle.

I'd recognized the bear sounds because Flynn had made them for me, teaching me what to listen for…

A rush of warmth swelled inside me, stinging my eyes with tears, sure peace flooding my heart and mind. No beast lurked in the woods, circling and teasing the mad man clutching his rifle in his hands.

Flynn hadn't died. He'd come to save me.

33

FLYNN

I groaned, the choked noise from my throat rousing me from empty darkness. Thinking I'd slept well for the first time in months, I rolled, and pain slammed into my head like an avalanche, dizzying my brain like I tumbled end over end.

My fingertips found wetness on my head, and I clenched my eyes tight against the throbbing inside my skull.

What had happened—

Saige.

Gunshot.

I pushed onto my hands and knees, realizing I'd sprawled across Brock's stoop. Blinking brought his empty cabin into focus.

"Saige?" I croaked, trying and failing to blink the pain away.

Sitting back onto my haunches and grimacing, I turned my head, the failing light unhelpful in allowing me to look over the homestead.

"Saige!" I hollered—she didn't answer.

Gunshot... I touched my head again, the sting of my

fingers sliding over a groove along the side of my head, gritting my teeth. I'd been shot. A mere flesh wound, but enough to rattle my brain and make me bleed more than was healthy.

Cold settled into my gut like a hard freeze, turning all life brittle. The pain numbed. My teeth grit tight as I realized what had happened.

Pa.

The bastard had taken what no longer belonged to him. Regardless of the pity I might have felt for him from the words in Ma's journal, he wouldn't live out the week.

My wound had crusted over along the edges, but blood still seeped enough I knew they hadn't been gone long.

He would attempt to take her home, but he wouldn't get far.

Saige would slow his steps, erasing whatever lead he had on me.

Teeth clenched, I pushed to my feet, grasping the doorjamb in a death grip, waiting for the dizziness to fade.

I had nothing but a knife at my hip and the pistol I'd found, which meant a close-up fight. Stealth would be key, something I excelled at. Tracking wouldn't usually be an issue, but darkness hovered, promising to slow my steps.

Pa hated traveling at night, hated the shadows that offered predators a place to hide, a way to sneak up on its prey.

Pa had become my prey, and hunting had been one thing he'd taught me well. He'd done so in order to make me the responsible party for putting food on the table—and I would use those lessons to my advantage.

I needed to take back my life I'd lost at ten. Needed to protect Saige like I couldn't my mother. No more being a victim and running off, scampering like a hare from Dog.

I'm the aggressor—I'm the predator in the night.

Pa's day of reckoning had come, and I would be the animal toying with its prey, taking vengeance for the ones he'd hurt. He'd taught me fear, and he would taste its bitterness before drawing his last breath.

Need to rush out to rescue Saige tensed my muscles, but cold calm descended. Rational thinking demanded I wait for light. I needed a plan—recklessness would only end in death, and not the one I wanted responsibility for.

Waiting for morning sat like a rancid carcass in my gut, churning and jerking my eyes open every time they drooped. Sprawled on Brock's bed, my head cleaned and bandaged, hands on my chest, I lay in the dark, thinking on how I would end Pa.

It wouldn't be quick.

It wouldn't be a peaceful death.

The pistol wouldn't do, and while the knife would inflict wounds enough to bleed him out, I wanted my hands on him. Bringing back the nightmares of his childhood. Wrecking his brain, taking him past the point of sanity.

I wanted him to taste the fear of a five-year-old child who'd disappointed his Pa and sat waiting his punishment. I wanted him to feel the twisting stomach of a young wife who'd burned dinner. Who'd failed him repeatedly, no matter how hard she'd tried to please her husband.

Pa had taught me well, but Ma had left me an additional gift of knowledge, and I would use it to manipulate the man who should have sheltered me, who should have loved me.

At the first hint of the sunrise, I rolled from the bed, my jaw aching from clenching against the throb in my head. I ate the last two cans of stew. Drank down the rest of the river's water we'd brought up the day before.

Sustenance to see me through the hours of hiking ahead of me.

I'd promised Ma to look after her bastard husband—and I wouldn't fail. I would see him straight to the depths of hell where his soul deserved to rot.

34

SAIGE

Every snap of a twig through the long night hours lessened Callan's hold on sanity. He stood with his back to the fire, to me, and had my hands and ankles not been bound, I'd have grabbed up the closest rock and went after him.

But tension rode his shoulders, kept him on alert. His head jerked side to side at every whisper of wind through the trees. Every rustle of leaf litter. Every sound emitted by the creatures of the night—including the quiet snuffling of the beast haunting him. Stalking around us.

I hunkered against the cold, ears straining for another of Flynn's bear sounds. Not having heard them from a real bear, I didn't know his accuracy—but from Callan's reaction, I expected he mimicked the beast perfectly.

But I knew it was Flynn. I recognized the deep timbre of his voice, the one that sent shivers over my skin not nearly enough times.

Giggles shook through me as Callan blasted bullets into the darkness, his curses ringing through the night.

As the sky lightened, the cat-and-mouse game Flynn

played ended in silence. Gone to his fear, Callan didn't even kick out the fire he'd kept blazing throughout the night. Didn't take the time to untie my ankles to replace my leash —he simply cut the rope away.

"Walk."

One simple command, an easy one to follow in mind, but not with my feet.

My head still ached, and the exhaustion from being awake all night weakened my legs. Callan pointed with his rifle, and I stumbled ahead of him, my gaze darting from left to right, desperate for Flynn to make his presence known, to end the nightmare ensnaring me.

But he had a knife and pistol to Callan's powerful rifle. He wouldn't rush us like a madman, like a threatened animal needing to protect its young.

No. He'd tracked us down. He would hunt as his Pa had taught him. Waiting for the perfect opportunity to draw blood. End life.

But would he after learning the truth of his father? Would the softness I'd see in Flynn, the empathy he'd gained from his mother, be enough to spare the man who'd hurt him and the two women he loved?

I dragged my feet. Stumbled a time or ten to slow our progress northward.

Twice, Callan slammed the butt of his rifle against me when I'd gone down, but neither time drew Flynn out.

Had I been wrong about the noises in the night? Surely Flynn would have come running if he'd seen Callan hit me in such a way.

Doubt crept in along with heightened exhaustion, buzzing my ears and hazing my vision. Tears pricked my eyes at the thought Flynn still lay dead, sprawled in the cabin's doorway, that his heart lay quiet, his lungs emptied.

That an actual beast prowled after us.

I didn't doubt something followed, waiting for the right time to take its dinner. Callan's continued alertness, his darting gaze, the hairs on my neck rising time and again... Something hunted us. Something intent on drawing blood. And with every passing hour, my own hold on reality warped, same as Callan's.

We didn't speak, but the shroud of darkness he emanated over me turned to fear rather than icy dread.

Mutterings behind me rose and fell, indistinct words, whisperings that raised the hairs on my arms and I found similar inarticulate words, thoughts, pouring from my parched lips.

Hunger clenched at my stomach, but we plodded ever northward, without stopping. No water since the day before meant dehydration and a throb in my temples, but still the body eventually required to empty its bladder.

"Need to stop," I rasped out to Callan over my shoulder.

The wildness of a scared animal held sway over his usually guarded eyes as he shook his head.

"I'm going to pee myself."

"Walk." He growled the word, seemingly more animal than man.

My steps grew painful from the fullness of my bladder, and I whimpered, lower lip between my teeth, desperate to hold it in.

A bird squawked, taking to flight mere feet ahead of me, and I shrieked, wet heat pouring down my leg. Soaking the pants.

"Oh!" My eyes stung as I stumbled to a stop—and Callan slammed his rifle butt between my shoulder blades.

"Walk!"

Sobs choked my throat. I stumbled onward, wetness

seeping into my boots, goosebumps raising on my arms and legs as the urine-soaked pants cooled. Wet. Cold. Smelling of piss…

Would it draw the beast out?

Darkness began to take over the sky, and we still hadn't reached the homestead.

"Fucking woman…so fucking slow."

Head down, I plodded onward, ignoring Callan's mutterings. Of course, I walked slowly, my mind consumed with dread, every step lessening my hope Flynn followed.

Branches snapped to our left, and I went to my knees as Callan swung his rifle, a bellow leaving his lungs.

Two shots.

Silence.

Nothing stirred through the brush from my vantage point. Still, Callan sighted through the trees, his breaths heavy through his nose.

"Goddamn bear. Fucking piece of shit." He spewed a few more curses. "Show yourself, goddamnit!"

My pulse throbbed in my ears, rushing blood with a steady thump.

Another shot, but from the hip, unaimed. Hoping to scare away whatever stalked after us.

"Get up." Callan booted my ass, and I struggled to stand, tears on my face, snot running from my nose. Heavy weight lay on my shoulder, and all I wanted to do was sink into the earth.

Become one with the soil.

Decay until nothing but my bones remained.

Flynn.

Memories of his mossy-green eyes blazing with lust filled my mind. Love. Roughened hands offering tender caresses. Fingertips. Lips. Wet tongue and sharp teeth.

Get up.

I stood on trembling feet and shuffled forward, Callan's heavy footfalls behind me. So tired. Hungry.

Cold.

My teeth clattered, and I tucked my elbows in tight, unable to wrap my arms around me due to my bound wrists. Another step.

Another.

Callan muttered something about the fucking daylight giving out, a steady stream of fucks and goddamnits following after. "Not going to make it."

The cold seeped deep into my gut, my bowels, no matter how I attempted to cling to my memories of my love.

Another night without shelter. Another night exposed to the elements, without protection from the beast lurking at the back of my mind. Claws and sharp teeth. A massive brute strong enough to swipe my head clear from my body.

Callan started a fire while I huddled against a rock, gaining a bit of strength of mind, having something solid pressing into my spine. He took up his wide stance across the fire from me, and I closed my eyes, ignoring the dried snot and tears tightening the skin of my face. The stench of urine wafted up, pungent and sharp.

I'd become nothing more than a filthy animal, scared for its life.

A rustling of leaves...a thump...

My eyelids popped open.

Callan jerked his rifle up, sighting over my shoulder, over the rock. "Fucking bear."

Eyes wide and jaw tight, I waited for the loud crack, the shattering of the growing night.

Boom!

I shrieked as movement shadowed at a tree behind Callan. Bulk. Darkness.

"Mother fucking—" Callan shot again, the bullet ripping through the woods at my back.

Silent, the beast approached behind my husband, the surety of death stealing my breath, my ability to make a sound. Hulking, broad shoulders. Auburn hair a wild mess. A wildling grown to a man of the wilds, face streaked with blood and dirt. Firelight reflected off the blade in his hand.

Not a bear—but a beast intent on killing.

"Flynn," I choked out a whisper.

Callan spun with a roar, but Flynn already threw himself forward. The knife clanged against the rifle's barrel, and the two men flew backward into the fire, scattering wood and embers.

The rifle spun off into the grass as Callan grasped his son's hand, keeping the knife from stabbing into his chest.

"Flynn!" I shrieked, scrambling out of their way as life suddenly kicked my body into motion, but he didn't glance my way, didn't take his cold gaze off the man he grappled with.

Neither spoke, but animalistic grunts, growls, erupted from both.

Callan released his hold with one hand and clobbered Flynn against the side of the head.

The knife fell from Flynn's hand, and Callan shoved against him, taking advantage of the stunning blow. He rolled his son beneath him, but Flynn jerked his knee up high, slamming into his Pa's back.

A grunt, a few fists, and they rolled again.

The knife lay beside a large stick, flickering with flames.

My insides stilled.

I picked up the knife, clutched it in my bound hands—

sure and steady. Unwavering. My mind seeing what needed done. How to avenge Flynn's Ma. Myself.

Him.

Callan sat atop my love, same as Flynn had done to him in the cabin. Raining fists. The smacking of flesh, the splattering of blood drawing me closer.

Flynn slapped at Callan. Landed a blow enough to stagger his father's punches.

I raised the knife. Met Flynn's gaze over his Pa's shoulder.

Feral animal. Wildling...

Teeth clenched, I slammed the knife downward, ripping into Callan's clavicle.

He grunted, and Flynn slammed his fist into the temple above the pommel still clutched in my hands.

Callan flew to the side, ripping the blade from my hands, and I stumbled away, falling in my determination to keep my focus on the men.

Flynn scrambled atop Callan, yanking his knife free. "You don't deserve someone so precious," he hissed. "Perfection. Beauty." Flynn flipped the blade in the air, grasping the pommel as it landed in his open palm. "You're a worthless piece of shit—just like your Pa claimed. Only thing you ever did worth a shit in your life was give Ma the gift of me. She said as much—and I fucking agree."

One swipe of Flynn's arm opened Callan's cheek.

"Son," Callan rasped out.

"No." Flynn swiped his other cheek. "You don't deserve to call me that."

"Saige," Callan groaned out, trapped beneath Flynn's thighs, unable to move, and I crawled closer, needing to see his face. Watch his eyes. See the blood... Needed to watch as my love defended the weak. Took down the once mighty.

"You don't talk to her." Flynn cracked the pommel against Callan's temple. "Don't get to fucking look at her!" He punched, whipping Callan's head to the side, his glassy eyes facing my way.

Flynn grasped Callan's chin and righted his head, leaning down to hiss in his face. "You don't get to touch Saige every again. She's mine. Mine to hold, mine to kiss, mine to fuck."

A slow blink, and Callan's lips went slack as though he sought words.

Flynn's arm raised to the side, and a solid thump sounded as he brought it smashing down, arching Callan's back. Flynn held his focus—and stabbed his Pa in the side again.

Another grunt passed my husband's lips.

"Mine," Flynn whispered and stabbed again.

Two predators had come together in a loud clash, and at the falling of one, silence descended.

I stared. A statue, unmoving.

Breath held.

Flynn did the same atop his father. Their gazes locked.

Quiet ruled the wilderness. No breeze, no rustling of dying leaves, or sounds of small critters.

A gasp ripped from Callan's lungs. Another. And still, Flynn didn't move.

"I hope you rot in that hell you thought you escaped when you left California."

Callan whimpered, his chest rising sharply—and falling still.

Three heartbeats thumped in my ears. Five. Seven.

A shuddering sigh rippled over my husband's prone form, his body going lax.

He's gone.

I lifted my focus to Flynn who still hunched over his father as though he teased, expected his Pa to laugh in his face, rise up to hit him, abuse the little boy's heart that beat in his son's chest.

"Flynn," I whispered.

He dragged his focus my way.

Blinked, his quick inhale filling the silence.

"Saige." A quick scuttle on his knees brought him kneeling to my side, and he sliced through the ropes around my wrist with the bloody blade. His hands trembled as he ripped at the rope's remnants until they fell to the ground between us.

My Flynn, my love, peered into my eyes, such warmth, such protective heat in his gaze, I whimpered, grasped at his beard, and drew him toward me. He tasted like dirt and heaven. Wildness and need.

My body's urge to have him caught my breath, smearing arousal between my cold thighs.

"Saige," he groaned into my mouth, his hands grasping at my upper body, pulling me in tight.

I stank of urine, fear, and body odor, but Flynn didn't seem to notice or care.

"Tell me he didn't hurt you," he whispered harshly, pushing me onto my back and prowling atop me. "Tell me he didn't touch what belongs to me."

"He didn't."

A rush of fumbling kisses, grasping hands...

The sweats ripped down my legs, off my ankles, and Flynn returned. "Mine."

"Yes—"

He shoved into my body with one thrust of his hips, and I shrieked, my back bowing off the ground. "Flynn! Oh, God!"

Rough hands grasped my thighs and spread them wide. Fingers bruising—and I fed off it like an animal starved for days.

"Mine," he grunted, slamming against my cervix. "Mine."

I grabbed hold of his hair, held his lust-filled gaze, and rose to meet his every thrust.

My wildling. My man. My love.

35

FLYNN

D irty.
  Sweaty.

Incredibly tight—wet.

My mind roared as I breathed her in, the sharp stench of piss, the coppery tang of blood on my tongue, the sweetness of her breath panting against my lips.

My woman. *Mine.*

I slammed into her over and over, unable to go slow or gentle—but I held her gaze, anchored my soul to the earth in her eyes as blood lust thrust me forward. Taking. Claiming what finally belonged to me.

Her tight heat clamped around me, and she let out a cry, her head tipping back, offering her neck.

Growling, I latched onto her soft skin. Fucked into her over and over as her sweet pussy milked around me, her cries tightening my balls against my body. A rush of tingles along my spine—and I came with a roar, cum bursting from my cock, shooting deep inside her.

Fucking mine.

I grunted, fucked, groaned, and shuddered with every

spurt of release. Panting, I finally stilled, Saige's arms and legs clutching me close.

No words came to mind, nothing but pure fucking elation.

Licking along her salty jaw, I groaned as one last jerk of my cock shoved deep inside her body rippled a shudder through me.

Saige wound her fingers in my hair, pulled at the tie hanging on the ends of my long strands, tugging it free. With a sigh, she buried her hands in my hair and pulled me in close.

"Flynn," she murmured against my lips, and I took her mouth, another rush of need to dive deep into her soul swelling my heart.

"Love you," I uttered the feelings coursing through me.

She squeezed her inner muscles around my length, and I pulled away, sitting back on my haunches. Cum slid from her pink hole as it contracted, and I gathered up my seed and pushed it back in.

"You're mine," I grunted through my clenched teeth, fighting the need to fuck her clear into the dirt.

"Always."

I held her gaze and fucked my fingers into our combined cum, the pads of my slackened fingertips feeling her softness, the heat of her pussy that belonged to me. "Forever."

Her dark eyes held me captive, and I leaned down to claim her once more.

———

I built back up the fire. Fashioned a quick lean-to with pine boughs and built my love a bed beneath. She lay atop my filthy shirt, my bloodied sweatshirt acting as a blanket. My torso bare to the cool evening, I set to work dragging Pa's body into a shallow left behind by a fallen tree's roots a hundred or so yards west of us.

The freshly uprooted tree offered disturbed soil and rock to cover him in a shallow grave. Without doubt, some beast would find him, eventually. Hopefully, rip his carcass limb from limb. Feast on his rotted flesh and eventually shit out his worth.

No trace of guilt filled me as I turned my back on his grave. No remorse over the truth I'd helped to end his life by stabbing him repeatedly. Saige's stab hadn't been fatal— wouldn't have proven to be left unattended, either, but the sinking of my blade into his side, carving out with its jagged edge with every backward draw...

The second he'd breathed his last, his body going lax beneath me, his eyes glazing over in death I'd seen countless times in the animals I'd hunted, a need so primal, so deep grabbed hold of me, I'd taken Saige.

Roughly.

Uncaring of her state.

Blinded to the fact she may be scared. Might need tenderness.

But she rose to see me, her body welcoming me. Twice, she'd come around my cock, soaking me. Drawing me in deeper, her panted cries in the growing night rushing my blood to coat her in my cum. My scent.

She eyed me from beneath the lean-to as I built up the fire, flames licking high into the sky. Wood cracking and shooting sparks upwards. Yellow and red, flicking across her face.

Pink cheeks.

Parted lips.

I wanted to bury myself inside her again, but sat on my

haunches beside the fire, watching its light play across her face. My chest rose in time with hers, sinking back down. Rising as one. Emptying lungs in a simple dance of life-giving force.

"Mine," I whispered once more, seeking out her big brown eyes.

Her lips curved. "Yes."

36

SAIGE

I sat in the cabin by the fire with one of my tattered paperbacks in hand, but I couldn't focus on the words. Flynn sat on his bed—our bed—against the headboard, reading his mother's journal. I watched him more than I read the story of lust clutched in my fingertips.

A slight furrow dented his brow and had for over an hour, his lips pressed in a thin line. Twice, he'd come to me asking for help to make out a word of his mother's tiny scripted words.

Waiting for him to take a break, to share with me how he felt, kept my stomach cramped. Every night for four days, he'd sat and read into the evenings what I'd already told him, putting the journal down when his eyes grew tired, unaccustomed as they were to reading for hours on end like mine.

We'd returned to the homestead to find Dog rotting where he'd fallen, and anger had clenched Flynn's jaw while tears had rolled down my cheeks. We buried him that same day beside Flynn's Ma on the brambled hill, a peaceful final resting place where he could watch over our tiny valley.

My chickens had gone over seven days cooped up in their lean-to, and not a one survived their time without food or water. More tears, more small graves Flynn helped me dig.

He'd told me my little friends wouldn't have lasted the winter anyway and would have ended up on the table like Joc. Something Callan hadn't told me when picking up the chickens to bring to the homestead.

No more chickens, but I had Flynn. The one living being I needed like oxygen, the only one I couldn't live without.

He held me every night. Loved me throughout the day—outdoors, standing, sitting, in our bed. An insatiable man who lost himself in me time and again, claiming he would never get enough.

Guilt sometimes slithered over me like a dark shroud that churned my stomach, but I'd never felt more content. Never felt so happy, accepted, and cherished.

But would it last?

Flynn turned a page, his frown deeper, and I wondered what part of his Ma's life he learned. The last time Callan had hit her, mere days before she'd written she would soon be too weak to climb the hill?

Flynn didn't have more than a page or two left—the final entry, then.

My heart beat heavy as I studied his face, waiting for a reaction over finding the truth about his father in his mother's own words. That he'd been born with a silver spoon in his mouth, but his father's money made by shady dealings. An evil, lawless man. One worse than Callan from his first wife's descriptions.

His father had traded in skin, kidnapping small children, using them as his own before auctioning them off to the highest bidder.

He'd used Callan for his sick, sexual pleasure, calling him a faggot, telling him he ought to enjoy the dick shoved up his ass rather than cry like a pussy. His father beat him in-between times, and his mother showed no pity, a coked-out waste of a human who didn't spare an ounce of affection or attention for him.

Callan's father beat her to death in front of him, and at fourteen, he ran off, living on the streets in Los Angeles, whoring himself out to pad his pockets.

His father's men came for him, thinking he might go to the authorities with his anger, his pain. Learning of the price on his head, Callan hitchhiked northward, not stopping until he landed in Anchorage.

He spent time living off grid with an old-timer and his wife, learning the ways of the land, and once he'd earned enough to buy his own homestead. He'd wooed Flynn's mother, whisking her away to the vast wilderness as he'd done with me. Also desperate for love and attention, same as Callan, it turned out, she'd gone willingly, with hope for a long future full of children and love.

A few years in, she learned disappointment. At the first miscarriage, Callan lost himself to anger, blaming her for their loss. The second, he beat her for the first time.

She held onto their third pregnancy beneath Callan's fists. Her only son, her precious wildling—Flynn.

Unlike me, his mother felt empathy for the man who'd abused her for years. She'd begged Flynn to watch over his father. Keep him sane since she had hoped he would one day come to terms with his upbringing and blood.

He never had, and Flynn's promise had almost cost us both our lives.

Quietly shutting the journal, he glanced my way, his

throat working even though his face lay void of emotion—bland like Callan's had always been.

Hiding pain and anger, the two emotions that always earned a slap or punch—for both when they'd been young.

I set aside my book and moved toward him, my heart breaking for the emotions I felt sure coursed through Flynn. Curling up against his side, I wrapped my arm across his stomach and clutched him tight.

No words, just something, someone physical, to help ground him. I longed to be for him, what he'd been for his mother.

Strong. A rock to lean against in times of trouble.

"Why did she choose to stay?" Flynn finally wondered quietly, his voice rumbling beneath my ear.

I had no answer other than the truth of what she'd stated repeatedly. She'd loved Callan. Thought she could change him.

"She was a chicken shit," Flynn spit out.

"She was an empathetic woman who loved him regardless of his issues."

Flynn snorted. "A fucking madman, just like his own father. She wasted her life away."

We breathed quietly for a time, and since I didn't know what to say, I stayed close, hoping to comfort him.

"His blood runs through me," Flynn finally whispered. "I-I'm afraid that someday—"

I sat and clamped my palm over his mouth, his whiskers tickling. "Don't even say it, Flynn. You're nothing like your father. *Nothing*, you hear me? You have a heart of gold. You're kind and compassionate like your mother was. You believe the best, hope for the best."

"But I killed him without remorse," he whispered against my hand, his pupils wide in the dim light, the green surrounding them filled with emotion. "I'm a cold-hearted bastard who used a knife to carve out his own father's kidneys. And I don't regret it. Not one fuckin' bit."

I stroked his whiskered cheek, trying for a smile even as my eyes burned to shed tears over the pain he allowed me to see in his eyes. "You acted on instinct, protecting the one you love."

The furrow between his brows slowly faded, and he pulled me up onto his lap, our chests tight, his face buried in my neck. "The only one I love. You turn me into an animal, Saige."

"A protective one," I added, hoping to give him some positivity to focus on. "Again, like your mother. You look nothing like Callan, so I'm assuming you took after her in that way as well."

"Yeah," he murmured.

Silence settled, and I didn't push to analyze his thoughts, his feelings. If he wanted to talk, he would.

"His father called him a faggot, same as me," he finally said, his low voice quiet. Reflective. "Made sure he knew his place in life, that everything he had, everything he considered his actually belonged to his father."

Same as I'd heard Callan often telling Flynn.

Apple falling from the tree and all.

"Did—" I cut off, reconsidered what I'd been about to ask.

"Did Pa do the same things to me as his father did to him?"

I nodded, unable to voice the sick thoughts in my head, and the idea the younger Flynn might have been defiled.

"Never, thank fuck. Guess he wasn't a faggot after all, like his Pa always said." A heavy exhale sagged Flynn in my arms, and he pulled back, smoothing my hair from his face with his calloused hands. "Let me love you?"

"Always," I whispered with a smile, the tears dripping yet again. "Whenever, however you want."

"I want you beneath me. Sheltered. Never wondering over my love. Didn't think I was strong enough. Didn't think I would be able to save you..."

"You are strong, Flynn. You're a damn rock amid life's storms. You set me free. You set us *both* free."

The thought he might want to see the world now he had that freedom flitted through my head. Would he find me lacking compared to the women in town? Would his simple life, one I'd come to adore, to crave, no longer be enough for him?

He'd claimed he had no interest to go to town, but he might change his mind one day.

He lay me down on his bed, slowly removed all my clothing, and worshiped me from head to toes, obliterating the thought our time together would end.

37

FLYNN

Pa had been a jealous bastard. He'd gotten a woman who loved him, gave him the proper attention and affection he'd craved. He and Ma had spent a few years together, semi-happy except for the "dark times" as Ma called them, came over him.

He would frequently speak in his sleep, and when he did, he brooded for days afterwards, she'd written.

Eventually, he told her about his past. About his abusive father, his inattentive mother. She had hoped he would heal inside, had even written he'd become more tender. Vulnerable and open.

But she hadn't carried their first two babies to the end—and the fact Pa's fists came at her when she'd needed comfort most, damn near made me want to rip my hair out.

Then I'd been born. The love of Ma's life, her sunshine, and Pa took my presence as his replacement in her heart. He'd hated me from day one, seeing how Ma's face lit up.

She'd tried to keep her happiness over having a son to herself, but Pa's brooding had only made her cling to her wildling even more.

He began accusing her of loving me more. Feared she'd left him behind in her heart—and he pushed her away in his own. I was lucky he hadn't done away with me to be the only one in her life again.

Self-shielding, Ma had called what he did with their love, but she hadn't been able to help him overcome his demons. The wounds of his childhood came back in full force, ruling his mind, sending him spiraling even deeper as they struggled to survive out in the wilderness, far from society, far from the mundane every day things of town that distracted a mind.

She never gave up hope, even to the end, the final entry in her journal, she'd once again begged me to never leave him, to help him through life, to show him what true love was. Unconditional. Forgiving. Long-suffering.

I'd failed in so many ways, but I told myself Pa had crossed the line of sanity years earlier. He didn't deserve second, third chances. His fists and words had done enough damage, and allowing it to continue would only ruin more lives.

I'd made my choice—and I would live with it.

Easily.

Saige and I returned to Brock's cabin to clean the mess we'd made, hoping to make it appear as though the place had gone untouched since they'd last visited. Blood from my head had thankfully stayed outdoors rather than soak into the cabin's floorboards right inside the door. Thankfully, too, I remembered to lock the place up before striking out after Pa and Saige.

We laundered the sheets and stayed an extra day, curled in our own blankets on Brock and Jessie's bed while theirs dried. The sweat pants Saige had borrowed couldn't be cleaned, and we'd buried them back home before striking southward. The other clothing, she'd gotten clean, and we tucked them back where we'd found them, freshly laundered.

One last good study of Brock's cabin to make sure all had been put back in its place—including canned goods we brought from home—and we headed back northward, cross-country, same as Pa had taken Saige. But I made sure to cover our tracks in the event Brock and Jessie returned before nature and her critters erased them for us.

Saige walked beside me, clutching my hand whenever possible, as though fearing to lose sight of me again. Her small hand trembled as we came upon the second camp Pa had made, and even though I'd cleaned up before leaving the first time, she still recognized the small clearing.

"I just want to check..."

She nodded, knowing what I meant, what we'd talked about.

I'd already covered my tracks from dragging Pa's dead weight to the fallen tree, but I still found it easily enough. The grave hadn't been disturbed. Neither of us spoke while looking down on the dirt, rock, and branches I'd piled atop him.

No regret, but worry more of his blood ran through me than Ma's still poked at my brain, even though Saige had tried to assure me I was nothing like him.

Did our pasts define our futures, or did nature, Mother Earth, allow for me to become the man I wanted to be? A sturdy man of the wilderness, solid in knowing where he'd come from, where he headed. One who loved the woman gifted to him with all his heart. The kind of man who would move mountains, face ungodly beasts including other men, to protect what belonged to him.

I would be such a man—I *was* such a man.

Because of Saige.

I squeezed her hand and turned away, facing northward, ever onward.

———

For two days, we did nothing but rest and eat, the first happening more often than not because I'd worn Saige's ass out. Always wet for me, always finding pleasure in my body taking hers. She never said no. Never asked for a break. She claimed I never hurt her, no matter how rough I took her or length of time to finish us both off.

I lay gasping between her thighs, my balls spent, both of us sweating. Face buried in her neck as always once we finished, I breathed in her sweet scent, so damn happy my heart ached to burst.

Her wet heat still clutched at my spent dick, but I couldn't move. Didn't want to break the physical bond between us. If nature didn't call, if the need for sustenance didn't growl our stomachs, I'd have stayed put.

In my woman. Balls deep.

Content. Vulnerable as hell and loving every second of her fingers trailing up my back.

A low hum built in my ears, and I pushed up to plank, staring down at Saige. "She's early."

Saige pushed at my shoulders, her face flooding red even as her eyes widened.

"It's going to be okay," I told her, pulling out of her warm pussy, taking a second to watch our cum pulse from her body before she bolted.

The way she hurried to clean up, tug on her clothing while I sat and watched, raised questions in my mind. Filled my gut with fear.

Saige claimed to love me—but would she leave now that the opportunity came flying in?

Jessie's plane buzzed ever closer, and I forced myself up from my bed, pulling on my own clothes a bit more slowly than Saige's jerky movements.

I opened the door, scanned the skies to find the Beaver buzzing overhead—Brock flying rather than Jessie, who sat in the passenger seat.

Saige stepped up behind me in the doorway, and turning to face her, I held out my hand.

An obvious question in the action, one I let radiate from the deepest part of my soul and through my eyes I never used to shut her out.

She inhaled a shuddered breath, her beautiful brown eyes filled with doubt and fear—but she slid her palm against mine and gripped tight, easing that fear that had thought to sneak up on me.

"It's going to be okay," I told her again, and we stepped out into the daylight, walking together, our hands clasped, and hearts bound.

We'd discussed the story needed to cover our tracks. Simplistic, easy to remember. Pa had gone off hunting and never returned three weeks earlier. I'd gone after him, following his tracks, but lost him in the wilds. The big lie of the story only the three of us would know, since no one else had knowledge of my ability to follow a month-old trail.

I thought I ought to release her hand as Brock landed on the river, but Saige clung to me like I held the power to ease her anxiety, that holding tight to me would make everything turn out alright.

I prayed to Mother Earth that it would.

38

SAIGE

I clung to Flynn's hand, the other clutching his elbow, my stomach in knots, my throat tight. He claimed he would love me forever and hadn't one mentioned leaving the homestead, but what if Jessie encouraged him to go into town, report his father's so-called disappearance, and he ended up wanting to stay in the hustle and bustle he'd never experienced as a man?

The thought of returning to town, to people, burned my esophagus with bile, and I swallowed repeatedly while walking down to the river's edge.

Brock hopped from the plane to tie up the pontoons, while Jessie took a bit longer. One arm in a cast, she didn't help tie up, but climbed ashore with a grin on her face.

Her smile slowly faded as she took in how I hung on Flynn, her gaze flitting behind us for a few seconds as though searching for my husband and back again.

I'd lied to Callan countless times about my want for his son. He'd taught me well—and I'd been a good student. Lying to Jessie about my husband's whereabouts shouldn't be an issue.

Still, my stomach twisted up tight no matter how much I assured myself all would be well as Flynn had insisted ever since he'd rescued me from his father's clutches.

"Are you okay, Saige?" Jessie said as we drew near, the concern etching her face brimming my eyes with tears.

I managed a nod, and Flynn squeezed my hand, clutching at his elbow.

"Pa went off hunting a few weeks back. Never returned."

Brock walked up to his wife's side, frowning over my words. "Where'd he head?"

"North," Flynn didn't hesitate to answer, holding Brock's gaze.

Squinting against the sun, Brock roamed his gaze over the hills around us—mostly northward, but he glanced downriver, too.

Jessie's gaze seared the side of my face, but I couldn't look at her. Face hot, still swallowing against fear and bile, I knew she would read me like an open book. I took to studying my feet like she'd probably expect considering she'd only known the timid Saige from town.

"Saige, do you want to go back with us? Wait for Flynn to radio in when Callan returns?"

I hesitated too long—Flynn tensed beside me.

Glancing up at him, I found his eyes closed off. Bland and emotionless. But the tension rising off him, the usual excitable energy between us, lagged.

He feared my leaving as much as I did his.

"I'll stay," I whispered.

Flynn's shoulders shifted with his soft exhale, and I turned to face Jessie, my chin tilting up. We'd found our happily ever after, and no one and nothing would take that away from us.

The backbone I'd found through my trials straightened my brain out. "I'm not leaving him."

Jessie studied me long enough I shifted on my feet, and she glanced at her husband. Brock studied Flynn, turned to me, but I held still, forcing myself to hold his stare.

"You won't leave Callan or Flynn?"

I kept my lips clamped. Let them think what they wanted.

Jessie stepped in and wrapped her arms around me. "Are you truly okay?" She whispered against my ear farthest from Flynn, and I melted against her, all my fear, all my anxiety releasing into the cool air at her gentle squeeze, the lack of darkness, threat, in her nearness.

"Better than okay." Tears clogged my throat, and when Jessie pulled back, holding onto my arm with her good hand, she nodded as though she understood.

She shared a look with her husband before he nodded toward the plane. "Got a pile of supplies to see you two through the winter."

And with his words, just like that, I knew they *knew*. Didn't seem to judge or care, either, since neither mentioned Callan again.

An hour later, Flynn and I stood by our supplies by the river, Jessie's hug goodbye lingering. "Radio us if you need us."

Not when he returns. Not if he returns.

Just if Flynn and I needed them.

I nodded, and Brock clasped Flynn's hand.

"Take good care of this girl," he told Flynn. "She's a good woman and deserves the best."

"Flynn is the best," I stated my truth, grabbing hold of his hand again.

Brock glanced northward before meeting my forced

stare. "Certainly a better man than the one you came out here for."

"Yes," I whispered, my voice choking out.

He hesitated another second as though trying to read my mind, his dark eyes poking and prodding.

Jessie took his hand and tugged him toward the river. "Let's go, Mr. Rich Man. These two have work to do."

"Sassy vixen." Brock smirked and glanced between us once more. "Take care."

"Always," Flynn stated, his low rumble promising safety —and the type of care I enjoyed beneath him.

Shivers licked over my skin and stayed even after Brock and Jessie disappeared over the far horizon.

Flynn yanked me up into his arms suddenly, pulling a shriek from me which turned into laughter as he buried his face in my neck, whiskers tickling. "I thought for sure you'd leave me."

"I thought the same of you."

He pulled back, and I wrapped my legs around his trim waist, loving the hardened feel of muscle and bone wrapped around me. His hands grasped my ass as he stared at my lips. "Never leaving you, Saige. You're my woman turned wildling by the Alaskan wilderness. You came out here, fought to survive. Fought for *me*. I'm never letting you go."

His kiss melted my insides, my muscles. His tongue seduced in silent communication.

Love. Forever.

No matter what would rise against us.

THE END

———

ABOUT THE AUTHOR

Lynn Burke is an international bestselling and award-winning author. A stay-at-home mom, she's a lover of coffee and vino, and with three spawn and two fur babies underfoot, noise levels dictate the daily switch-over time. In her few quiet 'me' moments, she can be found hunched over her Mac, trying to type as fast as her muse spews hot stories.

You can find more about Lynn at her website: www.authorlynnburke.com